THE COMPLETE CASES OF
THE ARSON DICK

Leslie T. White

LESLIE T. WHITE

THE COMPLETE CASES OF
THE
ARSON DICK ™

LESLIE
T. WHITE

ILLUSTRATIONS BY
JOHN FLEMING GOULD

STEEGER BOOKS • 2019

TABLE OF CONTENTS

MATCHES IN HELL

TODD NAUGHTON, ARSON DICK, KNEW THE OLD MAXIM ABOUT THE USELESSNESS OF MATCHES IN HADES. BUT IT WASN'T TILL HE TANGLED WITH THAT TRIO OF FIRE-BUGS WHO WERE RINGING IN THREE-ALARM MURDERS WEEK AFTER WEEK THAT HE REALIZED THE OLD PROVERB COULD HAVE A DOUBLE MEANING—WITH A BLAZING KICK-BACK AT EACH END.

CHAPTER ONE
ARSON DICK

TODD NAUGHTON, hunched in the lee of the thundering pumper, glared at the tottering front wall of the Bilsky Building. While searchlights played across the gutted structure, tongues of flame licked against the night sky and smoke billowed from the windows to bend hungrily toward neighboring roofs, mocking the water-wall thrown up by the blackened fire-fighters.

An ambulance wailed into the night.

In obedience to the hoarse shouts of battalion chiefs, a dozen nozzles arched as many streams of water into the inferno, which returned most of it as steam and dirty spray. An aerial truck churned up front, started to rise as screaming sirens heralded the arrival of another second-alarm company.

Naughton cursed, and moved back to the police lines. There was nothing an arson dick could do until that smoky hell was conquered—nothing, that is, save keep his eyes open and his mouth shut. An ache of frustration came over him; this fire would be like the others—incendiary—but the evidence would go spiraling up in those coils of brown smoke, his reputation with it. He glimpsed a white helmet bearing down on him and braced himself.

CHIEF SLATTERY'S white slicker was black-streaked; so was his smoke-bitten face. His iron-gray mustache was singed and damp, but there was nothing smoky about his eyes. They glittered like buffed globules of case-hardened steel.

"Naughton!" he spat through blistered lips. "This is another one! Started like those other eight—and all within two months. That's an average of one a week in your district!"

He fired into a wall of flame.

The arson dick nodded, glum. Since Slattery spoke the bitter truth, there was little he could reply. There was no use trying to alibi or kid the Old Man; Slattery had been eating smoke since Naughton was a baby.

"I've covered every known bug in town," Naughton said between clenched teeth. "It's outside talent. I'm doing my best…." His words trailed off in the noisy confusion as Number 11 Company began laying out their lines.

A battalion chief bellowed for the Old Man. Slattery flung him an answer over his shoulder, swung back on Naughton.

"You're best isn't good enough! I've sent two of my boys to the hospital tonight—that makes nine since this damn series began. By God, Naughton, I don't mean to lose any more! Either turn in the bugs responsible for these fires, or turn in your badge! This is your last fire. Naughton—one more, an' s' help me, you're through!"

His eyes flamed emphasis to his words. Then he turned abruptly and tramped over the maze of hose checkering the ground.

Naughton didn't blame the Old Man; it was only too true about the eight fires. Within the short space of two months they had destroyed well over a million dollars' worth of property and—what worried Slattery more than any financial losses—had seriously injured a number of firemen. The conflagrations had all been incendiary, deliberate arson. Naughton's job, on the arson squad, was to find out how the fires were started, by whom, and to get enough evidence to convict those guilty.

That was the rub—evidence. In a murder case, a dick can search the theater of the crime. He may find the lethal weapon to trace; he's pretty certain to find something. Robbery is much the same—fingerprints, entry marks, or perhaps a trace of the loot. But in arson, if the bug knows his business—and Naughton had to admit these arsonists certainly were adept—the fire itself is the confederate that covers, or wipes out entirely, all evidence.

It was no trick to learn that these fires were incendiary in origin; they were much too perfect to be anything else. The timing—the theater-hour when the streets were flooded with traffic to hold up the departmental apparatus;

the too-casual arrangement of draughts that gave the flames a quick impetus; and always the air-tight alibis of tenants or owners who stood to gain.

No, it was no trick to know the jobs were arson. It was the how and by whom that stumped Naughton. The insurance companies were making their own investigations and voicing ugly rumors about collusion. The fire department blistered under the criticism and looked to the arson squad for its defense. So Slattery, when Naughton couldn't get results, had issued his ultimatum—"Turn in the bugs... or turn in your badge!"

A disturbance along the police lines caught Naughton's attention. He saw a short, fat man break free of the restraining officer and charge, wailing, toward the blazing building. His crazy rush, however, terminated in the arms of a smoke-blackened ladderman who all but heaved his hysterical catch into the ready grasp of the pursuing policeman. Despite the squawls and gesticulations of the fat man, the cop propelled him back to the roped-off safety zone.

Naughton scowled, went over. He recognized the dumpy figure as Max Bilsky who leased the upper four stories of the six-storied building bearing his name. Bilsky operated a suit-manufacturing plant. His blatant, gold-lettered sign that read *The Home of Klassy Klothes* had fallen before the second alarm went out.

AS THE arson dick came up, Bilsky was frantically shrieking his identity to the unsympathetic cop. The excited manufacturer spotted Naughton, whom he knew by sight, and clawed at him. "Tell him—the *gonif!*" he shrilled. "Tell him he's gotta let me by! This is my business, ain't it?"

"Was a business," the cop corrected, unimpressed.

Bilsky wiped sweat from his moon-face. "I'm ruined, ruined!" he wailed.

The cop exchanged glances with Naughton. "Yeah?" he breathed cynically.

Naughton squirmed from the clutch of the manufacturer. "There's nothing you could do in there now, man. Why the roof went down nearly half an hour ago! You're covered by insurance, aren't you?"

Bilsky emitted a strangled sob. "Maybe in part," he groaned. "I got some coverage with Transcontinental Fire. But I had a lot of stuff in there what wasn't protected. I'll lose my trade... *oi!*"

"Just hear about it?" Naughton queried.

Bilsky took his hat off to wipe the sweat-band with a grimy handkerchief. The glow of the fire found a scarlet mirror in his bald pate. "Sure I just heard! Me, I got dinner with my alderman and seats for a show. My wife she call the box-office and say, 'Maxie, Maxie, we are ruined...!'"

The cop looked at Naughton, and a sardonic grin toyed with the corner of his mouth; he was a veteran of this sort of thing and knew an iron-bound alibi when he heard one.

So did Todd Naughton. If Bilsky was with his alderman, the arson dick would have to look elsewhere for his evidence. He murmured a word of sympathy—it had a sour note, however—to Bilsky, and melted into the crowd. He elbowed his way through and circled over to the south corner where the police had a sort of improvised field-headquarters.

A hand touched his arm, held him. He turned to face a girl, and the man with her. "Todd! I've been watching for you—knew you must be somewhere on the ground. Oh, it's terrible, isn't it?"

Clare MacGilray came of a smoke-eating family; there was no morbid fascination for flame and sooty smoke in her.

Naughton nodded glumly. "It's pretty bad," he admitted. "Slattery tells me two of the boys were hurt. He didn't say who."

The man who stood beside the girl answered. "Knuteson of Number Seven was struck on the shoulder when the sign fell. The other one was Torrence. You knew him, didn't you?"

Naughton winced. "Young Torrence of Number Nine? Lord, yes! Hurt bad, Rolph?"

"I'm afraid so. Caught inside. Chest, I heard. Isn't expected to come out of it, poor devil."

Naughton's mouth tightened. "You'd better take Clare and swing over to the other side," he suggested grimly. "If that wall goes, the mob may stampede this way."

Rolph nodded. "I had the same thought. Perhaps we'd better shift now, Clare." He put his palm under the girl's elbow but she pulled free and grabbed Naughton by the arm.

"Todd, have you seen Keith?" Keith was Clare's younger brother.

Naughton frowned. "No, is he here?"

"Somebody said they saw him around. He worries me sick the way he prowls around these fires. I'm so afraid—"

"I'll keep my eye peeled, Clare. Now, don't you worry—" He stopped as he heard his name called. Turning, he saw a soot-streaked driver barging through the police lines. "Here, Clancy!" he shouted to guide the fireman.

The driver lumbered over. He was tired, and showed it. His rubber slicker was torn and his boots slopped on the wet pavement. The scarlet number on his helmet was bent double and his eyes were smoky and bloodshot.

"The Old Man's combin' the lines for you," he rasped harshly. "Get over to St. Barnabas hospital. Torrence has come to. He's askin' for you. He found somethin' in there"—he gestured toward the gutted structure—"before he got jammed. For God's sake step on it! He's... dyin'!" He sobbed out the last word and swung sharply away.

NAUGHTON SWORE. As he turned back to the girl, they heard the hoarse shouts of police officers trying to force the safety lines back. A strange rumbling came from the doomed building. Flame danced more madly above the tottering front wall.

"Get back, Clare!" Naughton growled. "Rolph, take her back of the lines. You can see just as much from there and this wall is about ready to collapse. They're calling off the boys from this side."

"But Keith—" began the girl.

Naughton waved her away. "I'll have the boys watch out for him. Now you two got to get out of here."

Rolph gently forced the girl back into the crowd as Naughton swiveled and elbowed his way over to a cluster of headquarters men. He cursed young Keith; the damned kid wanted to be a smoke-eater like his father had been before him, but he was only seventeen and too puny for the hard training involved. But he was Claire's brother and old Duncan MacGilray's son—and that meant a whole lot to Todd Naughton.

He located the lieutenant in charge of the uniformed coppers and asked him, as a personal favor, to have the boys try to spot young MacGilray and keep him beyond the lines.

"That damn youngster hasn't missed a blaze since he could walk," grumbled the lieutenant. "O.K., Todd, we'll ride herd on him."

Naughton had lost precious minutes in seeking the lieutenant, but now, having fulfilled his promise to Clare, he roughly shouldered his way through the gaping throng. As he neared the outskirts of the crowd, he heard the audible gasp from a thousand throats. He paused. Over the clamor came the harsh, half-scream of old Slattery... answering shouts... the measured thunder of the big pumper's mechanical heart... then a weird moment of calm during which brown smoke billowed skyward... and the roar of the crumbling wall.

Even Naughton was gripped by the scene. A hoarse bellow went up from the crowd, fused with the thunder of crashing masonry and the screaming orders of the battalion chiefs. Then, as though a million scarlet floodlights had been turned on, a hot glow lighted the tense, eager faces of the throng.

Naughton whipped around and charged down the street. He found his own car wedged against the curb by a double-parked sedan. He had to find a cop to help him move the machine and while the cop, at Naughton's angry suggestion, started to write out a traffic tag for the delinquent and absent owner of the double-parked, Naughton pulled his roadster away from the curb, knuckled on the siren and roared across town toward the hospital.

Churning through the traffic, his mind was on the injured fireman. He always hated to hear of any of the boys getting cracked up, but Ernie Torrence was his friend; it had been Torrence who had first taken him up to old Duncan MacGilray's house, the mecca of all the smoke-eaters in the district.

The sudden coughing of his engine jerked Naughton back to his immediate job. The machine sputtered a few times—and died almost in the middle of an intersection. Naughton swore savagely, jockeyed it over to the curb and jumped out before it had stopped rolling. The cop on the corner panted up; he had heard the siren. Naughton ordered him to call the official garage and have the "damn thing" towed in, then he ran into the street and commandeered a passing coupé.

Five minutes later they pulled up in front of St. Barnabas.

Naughton growled his thanks and charged up the stone stairs. He started to punch open the front door when he glimpsed three men run from the side of the building and dive into a cab parked in the shadow of the drive. He recognized none of the trio but something about their movements gave him the impression that they had sought to avoid him. He hesitated an instant, wondering, then with a shake of his head, pushed inside the hospital. It must be his imagination was getting the better of him.

NAUGHTON DID not pause at the information desk; he knew where the emergency ward was located from bitter experience and he headed down the gloom-filled corridor. He encountered a young interne coming out of the ward.

"Hello, Saunders. I'm looking for—" He stopped. The truth was printed on the interne's features. "Gone, you mean?" Naughton blurted, as though the other had already spoken.

Saunders nodded. "I'm sorry, Naughton. He asked for you. Friends, eh?"

The arson dick jerked his head, tried to cover up his personal feelings under the brusqueness of business. "I understand he found something—inside. Wanted to tell me about it. You know anything about that?"

"Not much. Hansen, the nurse on duty, was with him and got the whole story for you. I came in too late—he was going then. All I heard was something about Keith MacGilray. I suppose that's old Dunc's kid, eh?"

Naughton felt a queer nervous ache in the pit of his stomach. "Torrence was a friend of the Old Man. Where's this nurse, Hanley?" he growled.

"Hansen," Saunders corrected. "Ruth Hansen. She's downstairs. You duck in here"—he pushed open the door of an empty room—"I'll have her sent right up."

Naughton nodded, walked into the room and began to pace the floor. Had Ernie Torrence lost his life playing nurse-maid to young Keith? The kid was crazy about fires; he'd been raised on them. At the MacGilray home you woke to fires, had 'em for breakfast, lunch and dinner. Company was always connected with fire-fighting in some way; so was the conversation.

Keith wanted to be a fireman, but, by some fluke of nature, he did not have the build. Naughton had never seen Mrs. MacGilray; she was only a frail, elusive memory, for she had died when Keith was a baby. But it was a dead cinch that young Keith did not get his anemic physique from his father, even if he did inherit his love of the fire-fighting game from him. Old Duncan had been a giant in his day and he had been the toughest, shrewdest, and best-loved chief the department had ever had.

Naughton's musing was broken by the appearance of a girl in nurse's uniform who entered quietly on rubber-soled shoes. "I'm Ruth Hansen, Mr. Naughton. Doctor Saunders sent word you wished to see me."

Naughton bobbed his head. "Sit down, please. Saunders tells me you were with Fireman Torrence when he—passed away. I understand he left a message for me."

The girl shrugged, hesitated. She was young, giddy-looking—and pretty. Her nose was tilted a trifle, giving her a pert look, and even the severity of her starched uniform failed to hide the full-blown curves of her figure.

Naughton was not affected by her charms; he merely classified them in the course of an almost automatic analysis.

"It was hardly a message, Mr. Naughton," she said in a low, husky voice. "You see, he was in considerable pain and we had administered a hypo. He talked to me, but, I'm sorry to say, it was rather—well—disconnected."

Naughton felt the blood creep into his face. He sensed the girl was hedging, deliberately.

"Just what did he say?"

THE NURSE flashed him a full glance, then averted her eyes. "Oh, he spoke about getting trapped. It seems he was caught between a back-draught or something like that. He tried to crawl out of it and a brace of some sort fell on him."

"Did he mention any names? Did he see anything wrong in there?"

"Why—nothing wrong, no! He asked for you, of course, but I can't remember—"

Naughton crossed over to her chair. "Now wait a minute," he snapped. "Just what are you trying to cover up? I happen to know that he mentioned the name of MacGilray. Quit stalling, or you and I are going to have trouble!"

Color stole into her smooth cheeks. "Oh, yes, I had forgotten. He did speak of MacGilray. I gathered he was some sort of a chief at one time or another."

"Did he say anything about Keith MacGilray?"

She stalled quite frankly this time. "I can't be sure. You see, Mr. Naughton, I was a little upset. The man was dying." Her voice rose sharply. "What sort of an inquisition is this? I'm telling you what I remember! That's what you want, isn't it?" She was plainly defiant.

Naughton was puzzled. This blond dame was covering up for some reason. She didn't want to name young Keith. Why? Good Lord, nobody suspected the son of old Duncan of…. Naughton felt his heart pound. He tried to force the insidious suspicion from his mind. It was hellish! Yet—Clare had seemed unduly worried about Keith's presence at the fire. Of course they all knew the kid was fool-hardy, that he was everlastingly chasing the ladder-trucks in the hope that he might get a break which, in some unforeseen way, would bounce him into the department.

He eyed the girl. She was staring straight at him now and it was his turn to feel disconcerted. Had Torrence found something, something that would hurt young Keith, or, worse still, the Old Man or Clare? Was Nurse Hansen covering up to protect the very people he himself loved?

It was incredible, impossible. This blonde wasn't the type who would jeopardize herself to protect anyone else; she looked much too self-interested for that. And now she sat stiffly before him, waiting.

"Perhaps you are a little upset," he admitted at last. "But the fact that Torrence sent for me especially, shows that he had something to tell me. I'm working out of headquarters on the arson squad—"

She paled visibly. "A—detective?"

"That's it. Now I want you to take it easy and try to remember everything Torrence said. Everything. Whether you think it relevant or not."

"I told you all I know."

Naughton grunted. "I'll let you think it over tonight, and I'll see you again tomorrow. If you want, I'll have Saunders get you released from further duty tonight."

She shook her head. "I'm off at twelve anyhow. I'll try to remember, but I'm sure I've told you everything."

Naughton started for the door. "Think it over," he growled, and went out, the conviction Hansen had lied to him still dunning his brain.

CHAPTER TWO

THREE-ALARM MURDER

NAUGHTON CAUGHT a cab, gave the driver instructions to proceed to headquarters, then countermanded them two minutes later. He'd have a talk with the kid. Although it was close to midnight, he knew the MacGilray household would still be up. And if you had any connection with fire-fighting—from smoke-eating to adjusting claims for insurance companies—you could get a welcome, and an argument, day or night, from the MacGilray clan. They were that kind of a family.

Old Mac was a smoke-eater of the old-school. What he failed to know about hydraulics and such of the new era of scientific fire-fighting, he more than balanced with his knowledge of fires and men. His red-flecked old eyes could settle on a distant streamer of smoke and in five minutes he could tell you more about the blaze behind it than all the subsequent investigation would show. Even at fifty-eight—before he was permanently crippled by a falling timber—he could snarl his way up a swaying *pompier* with the best of the boys; and if you know the guts it takes to hook that slim, pole-like *pompier* ladder through a window and monkey up it a dozen stories above pavement, you can appreciate the old veteran.

But you can't direct a fire from a wheel-chair, and MacGilray went on his pension. When he blasphemously complained, the doctors told him he was damned lucky to be alive at all—which he was. The peppery old smoke-eater had retorted that he wasn't afraid of dying because hell was one fire he'd like to try his hand at quenching, especially before a lot of noodle-headed doctors got there and spoiled it for him.

So when Old Mac couldn't get down to visit his boys, they came to him in his little home opposite Number 7 Station-house. The older ones came for companionship and to reminisce; the youngsters for advice. They were all welcome. When Todd Naughton, as a rookie patrolman on the police department, had made a lucky pinch of a couple of notorious fire-bugs and was subsequently placed on the arson squad as a reward, an older dick advised him to cultivate MacGilray.

"You make Old Mac like you, kid," the veteran copper had suggested, "an he'll teach you more about fires an' the sort of swine that start 'em than you could learn any other way in a thousand years. And"—the sage had smiled—"you'll probably be like all the other young bucks that haunt Dunc's house—you'll fall for that girl of his."

Todd Naughton had both followed the advice and fulfilled the prophecy. He had gained Duncan MacGilray's friendship, and fallen—hard—for Clare.

He felt guilty, somehow, as he paid off the driver and dismissed the cab in front of the little brownstone house. Across the street the wide open doors of Number 7 showed the lighted interior of an empty station-house. Light reflected on the gleaming brass pole by the folded doors. Ernie Torrence would never wear out any more pants sliding down that brass shaft.

The thought of the dead fireman stiffened Naughton. He turned, trudged up the steps and punched the doorbell. As he waited, he became conscious of his own condition. He mopped his face with a handkerchief, and it came away black with soot. His hat was a soggy mass and his topcoat was damp and shapeless from the steam and spray. He hoped Clare would not be home and glanced over his shoulder to see if Rolph's car was around. Strict traffic regulations prohibited parking in the immediate vicinity of the station-house, especially across the street; the giant ladder-truck of Number 7 needed the whole width of the street to swing clear. Visitors at the MacGilray residence parked well down the block. Naughton knew Rolph's red coupé by sight, and when it was not visible, he concluded they had not yet returned from the Bilsky conflagration.

THE HOUSEKEEPER admitted him into the parlor where he found the old smoke-eater slumped in his wheelchair by the window, where he could watch the station-house across the street. MacGilray always fumed when there was a fire, but he welcomed Naughton with a greeting as sincere as it was profane.

There was something tragically incongruous about Old Mac in a wheelchair; it was like seeing a polar bear in a perambulator. The useless legs were carefully concealed beneath a plaid blanket, but from the waist up he was big-chested and massive. His sorrel-leather face was blocky, square, and his hair was the soft gray of hair born brown. Even his eyes had mellowed somewhat and were vein-streaked. His grip was hard and firm.

"Well, damn it, Todd, I'm glad at least one young pup had the decency to paddle over an' tell me what's happened. Bilsky Building, I hear? Bad? Anybody hurt? How many streams? Three-alarm, ain't it? Well, what in hell are you mopin' about?"

Naughton tried a grin. "Gutted it completely, Skipper." They still called him Skipper although he hadn't officially given an order in seven years. "Incendiary... worst of the eight."

MacGilray whipped his head around. His pale, smoky eyes peered from under a hedge of iron-gray brows. "Other *eight?* You think it's a series then?"

"Not much doubt about it," Naughton said grimly. "I've raked the local angle pretty sharp and haven't got—" He suddenly remembered what the nurse had told him, and added the word "much."

"Well, you got *somethin'* then," snapped MacGilray. "That's good. They ought to hang these bugs, or fry 'em. That would be better—fry 'em. Let 'em know what it's like to blister, to death, by God! Any of the boys hurt, I asked you?"

"Torrence."

"Torrence? Not Ernie, Todd?"

Naughton nodded reluctantly. "He went out like a— well, Skipper, like a fireman."

"By God!" MacGilray swore, scowling out the window. "Ernie! I was a pallbearer for his dad and now— Why, hell, he was in here only last night tryin' to kid me." He banged his hairy fist on the arm of his chair. "That's murder, Todd! By God, if a man goes out with a gun an' shoots somebody they call it murder, but when a dirty, dog-whelped rat sets off a fire like this where a lot of decent boys risk their lives and then die in agony, they call it arson. Arson, bah! It's wholesale murder! If you find out who did it, kid, don't you make no arrests! Don't trust 'em to the care of some dirty, no-account, crook-lovin' jury. You take that blackjack an' beat the livin' hell out of 'em. Take 'em dead, an' that's too good for 'em. Ernie Torrence.... By God!"

Naughton felt strangely uncomfortable. He was grateful when the front door opened and he heard footsteps in the hallway. His first thought was that Clare had returned, but a moment later a gangling youth stepped through the arch.

Keith MacGilray did not resemble his father in either build or manner; he was slim, rather pale of skin, and a little sullen. Naughton suspected this sullenness came as a result of an inferiority complex due to his physique. Yet, despite the discrepancy in stature, both MacGilrays had the same pale eyes, the same dogged set to their jaws, and a certain directness, or lack of subtlety. Clare had the same traits, in a gentler form.

The boy stopped when he saw Naughton, and the dick sensed the lad's surprise. "Oh, hello, Todd. Hi, Dad." To Naughton he said: "Thought you'd be at the blaze."

Naughton remarked casually: "Was. Looked around for you. There, weren't you?"

The boy gave him a sidelong glance. "Why, sure. Sure, I went over on the second alarm." He yawned carelessly. "You'll be kept busy enough with all these jobs, I guess. Well, I'm off to bed." He thrust his hands deep into his pockets and sauntered into the corridor.

Naughton pulled his face into a troubled frown. He scooped up his hat, mumbled something barely intelligible about having work to do and started for the archway. Old

Mac made no attempt to stop him. The shock of Torrence's death seemed to daze him.

KEITH WAS halfway up the stairs when Naughton walked into the hall and called his name. He turned with obvious reluctance and tramped slowly down.

Naughton said: "Come on out on the porch, kid. I want to have a talk with you."

Keith hesitated, opened his mouth to argue, but the detective shook his head, inclined it toward the room where the old man sat hunched in his chair. The lad shrugged, shuffled down the hall and pulled open the front door. He glanced over his shoulder, saw that Naughton was right behind him, and stepped onto the small porch. The dick followed and quietly closed the door.

"Keith," Naughton began grimly, "Ernie Torrence was killed tonight. He made a statement before he died. In it he mentioned your name. This is mighty serious, kid. I want you to tell me just where you've been ever since dinnertime."

The boy stiffened, took a backward step that brought his shoulders against the stone front of the house. "Say, what are you driving at, Todd?"

"I'm not driving at anything. I'm asking you a question. Were you in the Bilsky Building today? Come on, come on, don't try to think up an alibi! Tell me the truth."

"No!"

"You weren't in the building? But you were at the fire all evening? Right?"

Keith nodded stiffly.

"Came directly home from there?"

"Sure."

Naughton shoved close to the boy. He raked his fingers over his own face and they came away grimy with soot. He showed them to the youngster. "See that grime? Well, I was at the fire, too, but my face is black. Yours is spotless, but your brows and lashes are singed. You were in that building, kid, and Torrence knew it! You've gone someplace and scrubbed your face! Now I want to know—"

Keith tried to worm past him. "Lemme alone, Naughton! You can't bully me just because you chase my sister. What if I was at a fire? What darn business is that of yours? I don't have to tell you—"

Naughton caught him by the collar and shoved him against the wall. "Answer my question, Keith!"

The boy wriggled loose, made a dive for the front door. Naughton grabbed his arm, spun him around and slammed him into a corner of the porch. Keith continued to fight, so Naughton whipped up his open hand and slapped him smartly across the face.

"Cut it!" he snapped. "Where did Ernie Torrence see you tonight?"

"I don't know what you're talking about!"

Naughton knew he was lying, and the knowledge angered him. He thought of the Old Man, of Clare, and of Ernie Torrence, and so he brought up his hand again and see-sawed it back and forth across the flaming cheeks of the sullen lad.

"You dirty little sneak!" he growled. "You talk or I'll jerk you down to headquarters! If I thought for one minute that you were in any way responsible—" He drew back his open hand again.

"Todd...!"

NAUGHTON RELEASED his grip on the boy and turned to face the girl who darted up the steps, tiny fists balled, face aflame with anger.

"You struck Keith!" she accused.

Naughton bit his lip. He couldn't tell Clare that Keith might be tied into the fire; he had no proof and he did not want to believe it himself. While he fumbled for an explanation, the boy came out with the bald truth.

"He thinks I set the damn fire!" Keith blurted. "He was slapping me so I'd take the blame or something!"

Clare swayed back as though someone had struck her, then her slim body went rigid. "You… Keith?" She jerked around until her flushed face was close to Naughton's own. "I wouldn't have believed that of you, Todd Naughton!" she snapped. "Oh, it's contemptible! My own brother and you—you—" She choked to a stop.

Naughton jerked his neck. "Keith knows something," he growled doggedly. "He's hiding some—"

"He's crazy!" Keith cut in sullenly.

Clare pointed to the door. "Go inside, Keith!" she ordered crisply. "I've something to say to Mr. Naughton."

The boy shrugged, gave Naughton a defiant scowl, and sauntered into the house and closed the door. The girl turned, glanced at Rolph who stood embarrassedly in the shadow, then swung on the arson dick.

"I'm sorry to say this in front of Jack Rolph, Todd," she announced grimly, "but since I don't expect to talk to you again I've no other choice. I am shocked and disgusted to think that you would be cheap enough to take advantage of my father's friendship, to say nothing of mine, and try to cover your own incompetence by seeking to bully a confession out of a youngster like Keith."

Naughton floundered in his mind for a defense but the presence of the other man disconcerted him. Rolph was an insurance adjuster and in that capacity was tied in with the big insurance companies. He didn't want to start a rumor that might involve the MacGilrays; not, at least, until he was forced to in the pursuit of his duties. Lord, he hoped it would never come to that!

The girl was talking again. "Please go now and—it will be better if you do not call again. Good-night!" She turned sharply away.

Rolph looked at Naughton, shook his head in sympathetic understanding. "Just a minute, Clare," he said mildly. "Why don't you give Naughton a chance to explain."

Clare pushed the front door open. "I saw him strike Keith. There is no way he can explain that!" She flounced into the hall, and with a shrug, Rolph followed.

When the door closed, Naughton was already halfway down the steps.

CHAPTER THREE
FIRE-BUGS FOLLY

IN THE months that Naughton had been a regular visitor at the MacGilray home, it was his custom, on leaving at night, to drop in at Barry's Lunch Counter on the corner for a cup of coffee. Habit took him there tonight. Hunched over a steaming mug at the far end of the counter, he tried to settle his seething mind. The genial Barry, fat and bald, made a gay attempt at conversation but was quick to sense Naughton's mood, and soon left him alone and went up near the cash-register to peel potatoes.

Naughton did not feel he was in the wrong. Keith, he told himself, was withholding some information; whether it was evidence that implicated the lad, Naughton had no idea; he was, in fact, a little reluctant to dwell on that possibility. Yet Torrence had died with Keith's name on his lips.

Ernie, knowing the growing intimacy between Clare and Naughton, had sent for the dick on his death-bed. That was significant in itself. Then the nurse, Hansen, had tried to shield the lad's name. The recollection of those three men hurrying away from the hospital on his arrival leaped into the detective's thoughts. Was there a connection? Had someone reached the nurse, knowing that he was headed there? Grim thoughts, half-formed began popping in his head. That parked car that hemmed his own roadster to the curb… the dying of that same roadster on his rush to the hospital….

He spun off his stool and went over to the phone, got the garage on the wire, and had a brief talk with the foreman. What he learned was grimly suggestive. The gasoline line had been knocked loose; he had simply traveled on the fuel in the vacuum tank, and when that was gone, he had stalled.

After thanking the garage foreman, he called police headquarters. From the sergeant in charge of traffic, he learned that the officers working the Bilsky blaze had not filed their night's reports. However, the sergeant promised to find out the name of the individual who owned the sedan which had double-parked by his roadster.

Naughton hung up, spun a coin down the counter and barged into the street. He flagged a cruising owl-cab and snapped the location of St. Barnabas Hospital. The arson dick wanted another talk with Nurse Hansen.

At the hospital, he found that the girl had gone off duty. The serious-minded young lady at the desk refused to divulge Ruth Hansen's address, but after a brief talk with the supervisor of nurses, Naughton learned that she had a bachelor-suite in the Rowland Apartments on Sutter Street.

Luckily, Naughton had kept his cab, and in less than five minutes he paid it off in front of the Rowland. Again luck seemed to favor him for the big glass door, usually worked by an electric buzzer controlled by the tenants, was ajar. He paused at the mail-slots only long enough to note that Miss Ruth Hansen resided in 302, then slipped into the deserted lobby, and trudged up the stairs to the third floor. He knocked firmly on the door marked *302*.

It was opened by a short, stout man in shirt-sleeves. He held the knob with one hand and a tall, half-filled glass in the other. Ice tinkled in the glass and radio music blared through the open door.

Naughton hesitated. "I was looking for Miss Hansen's apartment," he said.

The fat man grinned. He was bald, with owlish, knowing eyes and blue jowls that made him look as though he needed a shave. "You found it, brother," he chanted jovially, stepping aside for Naughton to enter. "Join the party. Hey, Steve, tell Ruthie we got some more company." This last remark was directed at an unseen individual in the room where the music originated.

Naughton frowned, but walked in. He meant to get the girl aside; the last thing he desired was to broadcast the purpose of his visit. He passed through a small entrance-hall into a living-room. There he saw the man apparently called "Steve." The Hansen girl was not in evidence.

STEVE RECLINED in a deep chair. He was a fox-faced individual with sleepy lids and a twisted nose. He gave an impression of absolute boredom. "Hello, Naughton," he yawned. "What do you want to see Ruth about?"

The detective frowned. He had an excellent memory for faces, yet he couldn't place the expressionless pan of the man in the chair. However, it was obvious the latter knew the detective.

"It's a personal matter," he commented crisply. "Suppose you ask her to step in here."

"Aw now, copper, you wouldn't want us to disturb the little lady at this time of night, would you?" jeered the fat man who had opened the door.

Naughton spun on his heel, stiffened immobile. The fat man had traded his half-filled glass for a .38 automatic. The muzzle covered the arson dick's midsection.

Again there flashed across Naughton's mind the picture of three men scurrying away from the hospital. One of the trio had been short, dumpy; another—he whipped his head around to look at Steve again. Slim, lithe, a human panther. But there had been three....

Steve unlimbered himself from the chair. "Get those mitts a little higher," he drawled, "an' face the wall over there."

Naughton shrugged, complied. The fat man backed over to the radio and turned on more volume. The dick knew what that meant; they'd shoot if they deemed it necessary.

Steve frisked him with slow deliberation, removing his service revolver, his sap and bracelets. "We can use these," he commented, and handcuffed Naughton's wrists behind him.

"Was this party arranged for me," Naughton asked, "or did I butt into something?"

"It went off accordin' to the book," Steve admitted sardonically. "Now don't give us an argument. Just play smart an' you won't get hurt. Get tough an' see what it gets you."

The fat man chuckled. "Yeah, see what it gets you," he echoed, with painfully obvious meaning.

Steve produced a roll of adhesive tape from his pocket and jerked his head toward the chesterfield. "Sit down, copper," he suggested. "An' stick your pan up. I'm gonna tape your big mouth."

Naughton looked at the fat man's gun, and obeyed. In a moment he found his mouth painlessly and efficiently sealed.

The fox-faced individual surveyed his work with saturnine satisfaction. "Now, Manny," he addressed the fat man, "suppose you take our pal into the bathroom while I make a phone call."

The man with the gun steered Naughton into a small bathroom and shut the door, leaning against it. The radio quieted for a moment and Naughton heard Steve, at the telephone, ask the operator for Sherwood 2400. He went a little sick.

Manny heard it, too. He scowled, sidled over to the bathtub and turned on the water. The resulting roar successfully drowned out all further conversation in the other room.

But Todd Naughton had heard enough to confirm his worst fears. Sherwood 2400 was the number of the MacGilray residence. No wonder Steve had ordered him out of the room.

At last Steve punched the door open and beckoned them out. Manny pushed Naughton into a chair with his back to the hall door.

"You'll have to sit on this job until we get done, Manny," Steve explained. "Keep that damn radio down so the tenants don't send the janitor up here squawkin'. But don't take any chances with this mugg; we don't want to gum the works now."

"When'll you be back?" Manny wanted to know.

"That'll depend. We oughtta be set by daylight." He hunched into a slim-waisted topcoat, cocked a snap-brimmed felt over one eye and touched four fingers to his forehead in a mocking salute to Naughton. "Be a nice boy, copper," he leered, and went out.

MANNY TOOK a slow walk around the room, peering at pictures and reading book titles. Periodically, he whipped his head around to look at Naughton, but the big dick sprawled on the divan, helpless. At last Manny ducked into the kitchen but returned immediately with a quarter-filled gin bottle and a saucepan of cracked ice. He loosened his tie, set up the gin, the ice, and a fresh package of cigarettes, on a small end-table beside his chair, and settled down to wait in comfort.

The chair in which he squatted was directly opposite Naughton, so placed that Manny covered both the hall entrance and the detective at the same time. "Sorry you don't drink," he jeered, and upended his glass.

Naughton made a futile attempt to slip his manacles, but they were Peerless cuffs and Steve had ratcheted them tight. Failing, Naughton surveyed his genial guard.

There wasn't much chance there. The fat man kept him under nimble-eyed surveillance. Manny belonged to the deceptive type that looks sleepy and logy, but can get into action with the rapidity of a coiled snake. As for the gin, there wasn't enough in the bottle to give Manny a good glow, much less dull his alertness.

Naughton broke into sweat at the recollection of that telephone call. Sherwood 2400! Where had Steve gone? Why were they holding him, and where was the nurse? He couldn't fit Ruth Hansen into the picture. He was certain that Steve and Manny were part of a ring responsible for the Bilsky fire, and that meant the other eight blazes that had preceded it. Had Ernie Torrence stumbled onto some hot evidence? Was that why they were holding him? In that case, the Hansen girl must know about it.

His thoughts took him around in a futile merry-go-round. It just didn't make sense that the nurse should be a part of the ring; not the particular nurse that happened, by merest chance, to be alone with the particular fireman that happened, also by the slimmest accident, to have stumbled onto the only piece of evidence so far uncovered. It was fantastic, improbable; the element of coincidence was too strong to support such a hypothesis.

Naughton's bewildered reverie stopped abruptly. His eyes were drawn to a door directly behind his guard. It was stealthily opening!

Naughton snapped his eyes back to Manny. The fat man grinned, raised his glass in a mock toast and sipped the contents with obvious relish. Naughton scowled and let his gaze wander back to the door. Ruth Hansen was easing into the room!

She met his eyes and they begged his silence. She placed a trembling forefinger vertically across her lips. Her right hand was folded around the neck of a quart milk bottle, club-like.

Naughton was dumbfounded, but her intent was obvious. He dropped his gaze back to Manny and found the latter staring at him with quizzical eyes. The radio was moaning out the raucous endeavors of a dance orchestra, but Manny had softened it in obedience to Steve's order. Suppose he should turn his head....

Naughton glared, edged forward in his seat. He banged on the floor with his feet.

Manny slammed down his glass and sat upright. "Hey, cut that!" he snarled. "Do a trick like that again an' I'll belt you on the konk!"

Naughton shrugged, risked a quick glance over Manny's shoulder. The nurse had sidled into the room and was now less than six feet behind the gunman's chair. Naughton tore his eyes away, nodded at Manny in token of surrender.

"That's better," sneered the fat man. "You won't get hurt just so long as you—"

The heavy bottle caught him squarely in the center of his bald spot! Naughton dove across the room as the blow struck, but his charge was unnecessary. Manny was out cold as a politician's conscience. Todd jerked around to face the nurse.

She had retrieved the automatic, but it hung limp in her hand. Her eyes, wide with terror, were riveted on the detective's face. Suddenly she loosed a quick sob and ran toward him, tore the tape from his mouth. "I'm afraid I've killed him!" she choked.

"I'll be disappointed if you haven't," Naughton growled at her. "Get the key out of my vest pocket and take off these cuffs."

She hesitated. "Are you—will you arrest me?"

"That will depend a lot on how you act and what explanations you can make."

SHE FISHED the key from his pocket with fingers that shook and managed, finally, to unfasten the cuffs. When Naughton's arm swung free, she recoiled and shrank in a scared little heap on the chesterfield.

"Where did your friend Steve go?" Naughton demanded.

"They're not friends!" she stammered. "Honestly, I've nothing to do with them!"

Naughton scowled. "This is your apartment. You lied to me once; don't try it again!"

"I know, I know!" she whimpered. "But they threatened me. I've read what happens to people that get into trouble with crooks. I was afraid!"

"You ought to read what happens to people that get into trouble with the police," Naughton reminded her grimly. "Are you ready to tell me what Torrence told before he died, or do we go down to police headquarters for a—"

"No, no! I'll tell you. Torrence saw this Keith running out a rear door of the Bilsky building when he first went in. He asked me not to tell anyone else but you. He seemed to think it was important."

Naughton winced inwardly. "Why didn't you tell me that in the first place?"

She avoided his eyes, stared at the inert Manny. "Three of them came to the hospital just ahead of you. First they told me they were detectives and I repeated the poor fireman's story. Then they took out guns and threatened to kill me if I repeated it to you. They knew, somehow, that you were coming. I was scared."

Naughton took a slow turn around the room. "Why were these rats waiting here for me? Or were they?"

She nodded. "I think so. When I went off duty at twelve, this Steve and Manny were waiting for me. They brought me here, tied me up and left me in the bedroom. They promised not to hurt me if I kept quiet, but I was scared. I managed to wiggle loose after I heard you come in and then when Steve telephoned—"

"You heard that?" Naughton asked quickly.

"Yes. He called this Keith. They are going to set another fire tonight."

"Tonight?"

"Uh-huh. Steve said something'd gone wrong, and that they would have to fire the Coast Wholesale Grocery Warehouse tonight and clear out. Of course I could only hear what Steve said, but I gathered that this Keith is either in charge or tied in with the ringleader. Steve talked as though he were just working for someone. They talked about me—and I was afraid they meant to do away with me. That's why I—I—" She nodded mutely at the unconscious Manny.

Naughton's mouth contracted into a thin, bitter slash. He picked up the cuffs, rolled his ex-guard onto his face and shackled his hands behind him, taped his lips with the same gag which had so lately sealed his own. A thousand questions burned in his mind, but he asked only one.

"Then Steve left here to meet Keith MacGilray?"

Her head bobbed affirmatively.

Naughton frisked his prisoner in the hope of recovering his own lost revolver, but apparently Steve had taken it. He turned slowly. The automatic was still held in the nerveless fingers of the girl. She offered no objection when he took it from her but crouched in beaten silence while he ascertained that there was a slug in the chamber.

"You've got one chance to undo the damage you've done," he told her bluntly. "Telephone police headquarters and ask for Captain Taylor of the arson detail. Tell him that I want a couple of men to come out here and take care of Manny. They'd better stay right here in case I miss Steve and he should return. Don't mention Keith MacGilray unless—well, unless I don't come back. Is that quite clear?"

She nodded. "And you?"

"That won't concern you," Naughton growled, and went out.

CHAPTER FOUR
MATCHES IN HELL

THE COAST WHOLESALE GROCERY WAREHOUSE, while only four stories high, covered an immense ground area. It was a gloomy, tri-cornered structure that would have been condemned by the fire-inspectors if the owners had not been so well connected politically. It presented a dangerous hazard owing, not only to its age and condition, but to its location, and the fire-department and the arson squad kept it under surveillance. Squatting on the fringe of the old section of the waterfront, it abutted the water on one side, a narrow street on another, and the third grimy wall faced a spur of the railroad. The original building had been brick, but additions had been added through the years that made it a veritable fire-trap. Fire-trucks could only approach by the single street; only the departmental tug, stationed several miles away, could attack a blaze from the water side.

Naughton thought of these things when he dismissed his cab two blocks from the warehouse and stumbled down the tracks. If Steve and his confederates were there ahead of him, they would probably have a look-out in the street.

He tried to keep Clare and old Duncan MacGilray out of his thoughts—without much success. Keith, a member

of an arson ring? Possibly the leader? The old man's ringing words seeped into his mind, crowding out all else.
"Don't make no arrests!... Take that blackjack an' beat the
livin' hell out of 'em, kid!... Take 'em dead, an' that's too
good for 'em!" Would the blasphemous old smoke-eater
say the same thing if he believed his own son implicated?
Naughton thought he would. But Clare....

Freight cars dotting the spur allowed Naughton to
approach without much danger of being spotted. He stole
a glance at his wrist-watch. The luminous dial put the time
at two thirty. The warehouse watchman should be starting
his semi-hourly tour about now. Then Naughton rounded
the boxcar nearest the loading-platform and glimpsed the
lighted window of the watchman's office.

A high fog blanketed the sky. Keeping well in the shadows, Naughton boosted himself onto the platform and
rubber-heeled toward the office. He wanted to catch the
watchman before he started his rounds.

Down the Bay he heard a ferry whistle for the right-of-
way, and somewhere up the tracks a yard-engine's bell
tolled monotonously. Naughton braced his shoulders,
unlimbered the automatic and moved quickly to the office
door. To his surprise, he found it ajar.

Remembering the last half-open door that had lured
him into a neat trap, he moved warily. He thumbed the
safety off the gun, kicked the door open the rest of the way
and sprang aside. He was not challenged.

Inside, he found the reason.

The watchman, a bony old pensioner, sat mutely against
the wall opposite the door, legs grotesquely straddled apart,
bloody head bunched forward on has chest He had been
dead only minutes. The time-clock had apparently been
torn from his shoulder for the strap lay on the floor beside

him, but the clock itself was gone. Evidently the killers were somewhere in the great storeroom beyond.

There was a telephone on the battered little desk within arm's length; a brief call and Naughton could have the district surrounded by police officers.

"Don't trust 'em to the care of a dirty, no-account, crook-lovin' jury, kid...."

Naughton remembered. He deliberately turned his back on the instrument and eased open another door that led into the vast darkness of the warehouse. Dank, stuffy air fanned into his face. The smell of spices, wooden packing cases, the indescribable odor of tens of thousands of cans, sacks of sugar, molasses, vinegars.... What a hell would be loosed if a blaze started in this place!

A night-light glimmered wanly at the far end of a corridor of packing cases. Naughton, pressed into shadow, listened. The silence was heavy, threatening. He moved crab-wise toward the light.

"I don't expect to talk to you again... ever!" Clare had said.

Forget it, Naughton! Somewhere ahead of you are men who have just committed murder, who are going to fire this vast building! One of them is the brother of the girl you love but you've got a job to do! Keep your mind on business, man, or you'll be joining Ernie and that poor old watchman!

A GRIMY, metal-caged bulb marked the entrance to the basement. The big fire-door was propped open with a case of canned goods; propped open to make a better draw for the flames. Naughton worked closer. Sounds—furtive, suggestive sounds—stole up the stairs.

Those stairs would be watched; he couldn't chance them—not alone. But he had to get down there. He backed away from the opening, sidled on down the corridor. There had to be another entrance to that basement somewhere.

A cat darted out of a shadow-pit, startling him. Sweat beaded on his head, dripped onto his cheek like a tear.

And then he found an elevator shaft. The lift was somewhere in obscurity above, but heavy, inch cable offered a way down. Naughton hitched his belt, buttoned his coat and clamped his teeth on the automatic. Then with an ejaculation that was half oath, half prayer, he reached for the cable and swung into the blackness of the shaft.

Thick grease ruined his hold and he went plummeting down, down. A loose strand of wire pierced his hand; tore into it and out again. Then his feet crashed into the cement base with a jar that knocked the wind from his body. But his fall had been practically without sound.

He ducked under the slatted gate and found himself in a dim-lit corridor of packing-cases. Even without being able to read the printed words, he knew from the deep, rectangular shape of the boxes, the contents.

Kerosene! Thousands of gallons of kerosene piled ceiling-high; two five-gallon cans to a box!

He came to the intersection of two walk-ways. The murmur of voices was quite audible now, although he could not distinguish the words. Dropping to one knee, he inched his head around the bulwark of cases. A grim sight met his slitted eyes.

ETCHED IN relief by a light behind them were three men, their long shadows stretching toward his hiding-place. Naughton felt his pulse pound. He had expected to trap young Keith down here, but somehow, with the boy now in front of him, he found it difficult to credit his sight. But Keith was there and so was Steve. A third figure crouched on hands and knees before a long, snake-like ribbon that wound across the floor to disappear finally among the maze of boxes.

Although nearly a hundred feet away, Naughton knew instinctively what they were doing. That black, coiling shadow was an oil-soaked strand of wicking; a fuse, which would burn until it carried the fire directly to those cases of highly inflammable goods. From his position, Naughton was unable to determine whether the fuse led to the kerosene or to some other equally dangerous substance. Once ignited, however, it would give the arsonists just time enough to leave the warehouse before the whole basement would burst into a flaming hell.

Even as he stared, the bent figure raked a match on the cement floor and touched off the fuse.

"Run!" shouted Steve.

Naughton started to his feet. He meant to charge straight toward them, stamp out the fire and come to grips with the trio. But, abruptly, he froze immobile. For as the fuse glowed alive and the man with the match made a dive to join the already moving Steve, Keith MacGilray suddenly produced a gun and covered them. His words rang down the hollow tunnel of cases.

"Stay where you are!" he warned grimly.

The pair hesitated, paralyzed with surprise.

"What the hell!" rasped Steve. "Are you nuts? We gotta get out of here before that—"

MacGilray shook his head. "I've finally got you rats where I want you!" he shouted.

"Stool!" snarled Steve.

The boy edged around, menacing them with his gun, and backed toward the crawling flame.

Naughton, as surprised as the two firebugs, paused to see what the lad had in mind. Was young Keith pulling a fast one? Was he trying to play copper? A faint glow of understanding, of hope, crawled into the arson dick's consciousness.

Keith kept his gaze on his two victims and pawed around with his foot, seeking the fuse.

"Look out… the coal oil!" Steve roared suddenly.

INSTINCTIVELY MacGILRAY turned his head. All Naughton could do was shout a warning. The distance was too great for him to risk a shot in the narrow corridor. Helpless, he saw Steve whip out a gun and fire. Young Keith spun around and pitched against the wall of boxes, slid to the floor within an arm's length of the still burning fuse.

Naughton was running now. He heard a startled yelp of warning from the other man, saw Steve whirl—and then lead spewed at him.

Todd threw himself flat against the cases, steadied his arm and fired… once… twice. Then the pair were out of sight behind the boxes.

Naughton gave up all semblance of caution now. A wild exultation surged through him. Keith had been on the square. Perhaps he was dead, but he was straight! Naughton vaulted over the body of the boy and charged for the foot of the stairs.

He ran into a pool of flame!

The bugs had thought fast; they had dumped the contents of a five-gallon can over the stairs, over the floor, and over the tiers of boxes, then they had hastily dropped a match in the kerosene, throwing up a wall of flame to cover their escape.

Naughton leaped backward to drag Keith's body to one side, throwing a last shot through the roaring furnace as he did so. Simultaneously the big metal-covered fire-door slammed!

As the blaze licked and sucked at the cases, Naughton read menace in the contents. They were filled with matches. Millions of combustible matches, gallons of kerosene— and the fire-doors closed against him!

He whipped off his coat and beat futilely at the dancing flame. Oil splashed on his coat; it, too, burst alight. He dropped it hastily and looked above. The ceiling was criss-crossed with a sprinkler system. He jerked a box around, scrambled up to the pipes and beat off the valve-head with his gun. Hope flamed— and died as a weak, useless dribble trickled out. The arsonists had cut off the water.

A sudden fear clawed at Naughton as he saw the burn-ing oil seeping along the floor toward the body of the boy. Throwing his now useless gun from him—guns were no good when the very walls were likely to explode into flame—he scooped the inert figure into his arms and ran for the elevator shaft. That was their one chance.

Halfway to his goal, the lights went out! The main switch had been pulled! The basement was illuminated now by the flames. A case of matches burst ablaze with a loud *whoosh* and the acrid odor of sulphur rode ahead to herald billows of smoke. Kerosene fumes threatened to suffocate him even before the flames put in their claim!

At last Naughton made the shaft, only to confirm his fears; the elevator, with the power cut off, was useless, completely out of commission.

He laid the boy on the floor. Keith, he found, was still alive. Blood streamed from his head, but a hasty examination convinced Naughton that the slug had only creased the skull.

Todd doubted whether he could climb up the greasy steel cable and make good his own escape. With the boy it was out of the question.

He swiveled—and his breath seemed to sear his very lungs. The cases of matches were roaring and sputtering like Chinese firecrackers. Any minute the kerosene would go up. Now he caught another odor—the smell of burning sugar.

Out of the files of his memory popped tales repeated by veteran smoke-eaters. Burning sugar, rivers of molten syrup crawling hungrily along the floor, eating shoes, boiling the very flesh from one's bones. Intense, unspeakable agony, slow death! Better the quick finish of flaming oil than the insufferable torture of boiling sugar-syrup!

The boy at his feet stirred, rolled over and tried to lift his head. Naughton dropped beside him.

"Keith, Keith! It's Todd! Can you get up, kid! We're trapped!"

MacGilray tried, gamely. Naughton raised him to his knees, but it was useless. The boy put out one leg, only to have it buckle under him, send him sprawling. "I nearly had 'em!" he moaned. "I nearly had 'em, Todd!"

Naughton lifted him to a sitting position. "For God's sake, kid, what brought you down here?"

"Wanted to catch 'em myself."

"But why didn't you let me help you, especially if you knew who it was?"

"I don't know! Somebody big's behind 'em. Steve an' Ike an' Manny only work for somebody!"

Another case of matches ignited with a terrifying erup-
tion and blue light splayed over the scene in eerie shades.

Keith looked at the flames, and sweat pearled on his face,
but he understood. "Beat it, Todd! You can't get me out of
here!"

"I can't leave you, kid!"

Keith tried to shove him away, but the effort was too
much. "Don't be a damn fool!" he managed. "You got to get
the guy back of this. He's going to meet Steve an' Ike—"

"Ike is the man who touched off the fuse?"

Keith nodded. "Ike Wycoff, yes. This is their last job
locally. They're going to meet the big-shot for the pay-off.
I tried to play detective—you know why—but I wasn't man
enough."

"Where they going to meet, kid?"

"Ike's got an apartment—" He keeled sideways and lay
still.

Somewhere in the distance, a siren wailed. Todd Naughton felt an insane desire to laugh. This was the last fire of
the mob, and it would be his last, too. All chance of exit by
the stairs was cut off by the flames; the elevator shaft was
at once their only feeble hope and their worst enemy, for
the shaft acted like a great chimney and was sucking the
fire toward them. Soon the flames would engulf them and
roll up the shaft to spread over the entire structure.

He thrust his head under the gate and glared up the
shaft. It faded, overhead, into a vague blackness, but the
greasy cement walls in front of him were dancing with the
light of the advancing death. It was impossible, definitely
impossible! He had to discard even the thought of going
up alone on the chance that he might get help. He could
never beat those flames.

As his mind feverishly whipped from one impossible idea to another, there came to his ears the imperative bleat of a river tug. It was a sound that he heard daily; a part of the heart-beat of the river-traffic, of the city itself. But cornered there in the cellar of the ancient warehouse, the noise geared into a blank space in his brain, churning his thoughts into a new channel.

The river!

Only one thick, cement wall separated him from the river. Boats plied that watery artery, boats that delivered freight to warehouses such as this one. That was the reason for its location. Somewhere along the wall there must be an entrance from the waterway; there had to be, he reasoned frantically.

HE GLANCED down at the boy. Keith was limp, out. Naughton paused only long enough to orient himself, then started fighting along the wall, groping, squinting through a fog of smoke. The stuff burned his eyes, blinded him. Twice the flames cut him off, but each time he managed to circle the blaze by crawling over piles of cases, for the fire followed the open corridors, drawn by the suction of the elevator shaft.

At last he found it, high up on the wall; two great iron doors clamped by a heavy bolt. From it a metal chute coursed to the floor.

Naughton tried to struggle up the chute, but it was like climbing a wall of greased glass. The metal surface had been polished smooth by the rush of countless thousands of boxes and bags shot from river barges and freighters. He abandoned the attempt and turned to the tiers of crates. Working feverishly, he dragged a half dozen of them to the clearing under the iron doors, piled them into a rough pyramid and swarmed up them to his goal.

The bolt stuck, but using a case of canned goods as a maul, he battered it open. Clear air belched in to meet the advancing wall of smoke, only to turn tail and flee before the billowing fog. The new draught turned the tide of the fire, accelerated it.

Naughton saw his danger. With eyes stung shut, he managed to paw the doors shut and hook them temporarily. The smoke, robbed of its escape, engulfed him. He eluded it by dropping to floor level once more, crawling back to the shaft along the surface of the cement floor.

The blaze was already licking toward the cases of kerosene. Naughton glimpsed it and his stomach dropped. Once the flames reached those cans, sealed as they were, the resulting explosion would push the main floor clear through the roof.

He found Keith by sense of touch alone, for the place was opaque with smoke. Naughton blessed the many tips he had received from old McGilray; tips on how to conserve the few precious drops of air in your lungs, how to find pools of oxygen in a hell of smoke. He needed every trick of the smoke-eating craft to reach his pyramid of boxes again, but he made it.

Blinded, he groped his way to the top of the cases, jerked open the doors. The first cool rush of damp air revived him. He drank deeply of it before the rolling smoke chased it away and with his lungs full, dove back and dragged the limp body of Keith to the top, heaved him over the sill. He fell, rather than clambered, out after the boy.

For a couple of minutes they lay inert on a small wooden platform that ringed the water-side of the building. Smoke and flame clutched at them with hot, nebulous fingers, but

Naughton knew he had won through. Then he remembered the danger of the kerosene and crawled to his feet. He half dragged, half carried, Keith beyond the danger-zone, and propped him against a fence.

The lad stirred restlessly, opened his eyes.

Satisfied that Keith was all right, Naughton stumbled back to the little office on the main floor. Smoke had filtered there ahead of him and below he caught the rumble of fire. He grabbed the telephone and rasped out a curt warning to the operator. Halfway to the door, he noticed the body of the watchman. He couldn't leave him there to be cremated; furthermore, that poor dead body was evidence of murder. Hefting the corpse onto his back, he staggered from the building.

Two minutes later, the basement of kerosene exploded! Before the thunderous echo had faded, the Coast Whole-sale Warehouse was a flaming furnace!

Naughton left the dead watchman hidden behind a tool-shed across the tracks and ran toward the spot where he had left young Keith. The rich flavor of success was in his being. With Keith conscious, he would learn the location of the meeting where Steve and Ike Wycoff were to receive their pay from the man responsible for the wave of incendiarism; for the death of Ernie Torrence, and the watchman; and the injuries of the firemen. And Naughton knew they were going to pay, for he fully intended to follow MacGilray's grim advice.

"… take 'em dead, an' that's too good for 'em…!"

He reached the fence, stopped. Elation drained from him and the taste of success went sour in his mouth.

Keith MacGilray was gone!

CHAPTER FIVE
THE FOURTH MAN

TODD NAUGHTON slumped wearily to a pile of railroad ties. His first thought was that Steve and Ike might have watched them come out and taken the kid, but cold logic knocked that theory into the discard. It was unlikely, in the first place, that the bugs would linger at the scene of their crime and so risk detection. And granting they had, there would be no purpose in kidnaping the boy; they would undoubtedly have killed him where he lay.

To clear up that point, Naughton made a quick, but thorough, examination of the ground. There was no sign of a struggle, or a body. On the contrary, he found the prints of Keith stumbling along the tracks. Hope had a quick rebirth, and he followed the faltering impressions. They told a story. Keith had recovered his equilibrium as he walked, for the prints steadied, became longer as the boy apparently hit his stride. It was obvious that his scalp wound had been superficial; just enough, evidently, to knock him out.

Two hundred yards from the roaring building, the trail left the railroad tracks and disappeared onto a cement street. There it ended.

Naughton stopped, patted a tremulous hand to his blistered face. His skin was scorched, brows gone and the hair beneath his limp felt was curled ash.

The air was alive with the odor of smoke and the wail of sirens. Naughton looked back. A fiery halo ringed the gray-black pile of the warehouse. There was no use going back there. Slattery would be waiting for him. This meant the end of his career.

Had Keith double-crossed him? New doubts began to assail Naughton. Was the boy innocent, or had that tableau in the basement been just a gag?

Well, he had one ace-in-the-hole... Manny!

He yanked his hat down on his forehead and ran to the nearest intersection, hailed a cab. The driver was reluctant to receive such a filthy scarecrow for a passenger but Naughton chopped short his protests by flashing his shield. "Get going," he ordered. "This is official business!" He gave the address of the Rowland Apartments.

When the taxi skidded to a shuddering stop a few minutes later in front of the Rowland, a squad-car was standing at the curb. Naughton hit the pavement almost before his cab stopped rolling, tossed a bill at the driver and pushed into the lobby. He was surprised to encounter several reporters usually assigned to the headquarters beat. They advanced in a body, but he waved them away and took the stairs, three at a time. An uncomfortable premonition of trouble gnawed at him. Panting, he reached the door of Apartment 302. He knocked and it was yanked open by Captain Taylor, his immediate superior.

"Thank God!" Naughton gasped, striding into the room, "Was afraid maybe my man escaped."

Taylor eyed him grimly. "He's still here," he growled. "In the bedroom. Take a look."

Naughton crossed the room in three strides, and met Nunnally of the homicide detail coming through the door-way. The medical examiner was behind him. He shoved past them, stopped.

Manny lay stretched on the double bed. His wrists were still joined by Naughton's cuffs, his lips were still sealed. But he was dead.

He was not alone. The body of Ruth Hansen rested beside him. A blackish stain on the front of her dress told the story, at least part of it anyway.

Naughton's knees buckled. He grabbed the foot-post of the bed and jerked around.

Captain Taylor gave him the answer. "A girl called—I guess it was this kid—for she said her name was Ruth Hansen an' that you'd told her to get us over here. I brought Criss an' came myself. We found 'em dead. The girl was doubled over near the door, like she was drilled when she opened it to admit someone. This other mugg"—he indicated the deceased Manny—"was shot while he crouched on the davenport."

"Who did it?" Naughton stammered, and the moment the question left his lips, he repented it.

Taylor gave him a cold stare. "We expect that information to come from you."

NAUGHTON TURNED and walked unsteadily into the living-room. He picked a cigarette from a humidor, lighted it absently, and dropped into a chair. He felt, rather than saw, the headquarters men ringed around him, awaiting the explanation he could not give.

Lord! Had Keith—

"Who was this girl?" Taylor prompted.

Naughton sighed. "She was the nurse at St. Barnabas' Hospital who was with Ernie Torrence when he died."

The medical examiner whistled softly. "I thought I'd seen her before," he muttered.

"Well?" from Taylor.

Naughton explained. "I was at the Bilsky fire when Torrence was injured and taken to the hospital. He sent for me, wanted to make a statement of something he had seen. Before I got there this lug, Manny, and his confederates had reached her. They put the fear of death into her and threw me off the trail for a while."

Taylor scowled. "If you went straight out there," he grumbled, "I can't see how they could get enough start on you to scare off this particular nurse. How'd they know about Torrence making a statement?"

Naughton shrugged. "I went right out, but they must have known I was heading that way for they disconnected the gas-line on my car and before I even got into the car I was delayed by some damned fool who'd parked—"

He stopped, jerked erect. Ruth Hansen had told him the men knew he was coming, had warned her of his impending visit. They had torn his gas-line loose to detain him. Why not that car, too? It had cost him as much time as the broken line....

He dove off the chair and caught up the telephone. While the detectives stared, he called the traffic detail at headquarters. The sergeant on the desk had been as good as his word.

"That sedan," he said, "was registered to Sarah Wycoff, Forty-nine Thirty-six West Fourteenth Street. It was a Thirty-four Buick—"

But Naughton didn't wait to hear any more. He pronged the receiver, came to his feet. "No more wild-goose chases, Naughton," Captain Taylor growled. "You've got a lot of explaining to do right here, young fella."

Naughton walked over to his chief. "Skipper, you can't take this one chance away from me!" he challenged. "I'm satisfied I know the man back of these fires!"

"You know him?"

Naughton bobbed his head, lips taut. "I can't name him yet, but give me two men, and a gun—"

Captain Taylor looked deep into his eyes, then scooped up his hat. "Criss, loan Naughton your gun. You stick here. Nunnally, you can—" But Nunnally was already halfway to the hall door.

Naughton paused only to receive the borrowed gun, then followed the two veterans to the street.

Taylor took the wheel of the powerful car himself and as the engine thundered alive, he growled: "All right, kid, name it!"

Naughton pawed his way into the front seat. "Fourteenth Street West. The Forty-nine-hundred—" His words were lost in the snarl of gears.

As the big squad-car caromed around the first turn, the siren began its imperative wail. The streets were deserted save for an occasional truck. The headlight beams reached into the semi-darkness like the feelers of a great bug. Already the sky was suffused with the dull steel of an approaching dawn.

CONVERSATION WAS impossible, for which Naughton was grateful. Suppose the address was a phony? Suppose Ike and the others had already lammed? It seemed, as they hurtled through the night, a slim chance. But it was the only fragment left of the case. If this clue blew up in his face, Naughton was finished. He harbored a vague certainty that now he knew the man behind the string of fires, but unless he caught up with Ike Wycoff or Steve, he had no proof. And Keith…? He tried to shove the thought out of his mind.

The siren quieted and two blocks further Taylor wrenched the big car around a corner. "Here's the Forty-nine-hundred block!" he shouted. The headlights swept the narrow street in a wide arc.

Naughton clawed open the door at his side. "Look!" he yelled. "That Buick!"

A Buick sedan was parked on the wrong side of the street in front of a dingy brownstone house. Its lights were on dim and the vague outline of a woman was discernible behind the wheel. But it wasn't the woman, nor the sedan, that held the attention of the three dicks.

Etched in the glare of the police headlights, four figures moved across the sidewalk between the brownstone house and the Buick. Two men supported a limp form, half dragging it between them. The fourth figure, a tall, slim man, brought up the rear, hands hidden in the pockets of a topcoat.

The trio sensed their danger as the light struck them. The leading pair dropped their burden and made a dive for the open door of the sedan. Simultaneously, the machine started from the curb.

"That sedan!" Naughton screamed in Taylor's ear. "Crash it!"

Taylor nodded, braced himself, and swung hard on the wheel. Naughton was half out of the car when they smashed into the Buick. The impact hurtled him to the pavement, but he took the fall rolling. As he scrambled to his feet, he saw Nunnally firing from the running-board. Gun-fire snarled above the roar of locked cars. Headlights painted crazy shadows against the stone walls of the building.

Ike Wycoff was on his hands and knees in the middle of the street. Steve was shooting it out with Nunnally. The veteran homicide dick was firing as coolly as though he were practicing on the range. Taylor, half out of the front seat, was exchanging shots with the woman driver of the Buick who blazed at him through a shattered windshield. The still mound on the sidewalk in front of the house was Keith MacGilray.

The fourth man was gone!

Naughton limped to his feet and ran for the open door of the house. He cleared the figure of young MacGilray without a glance and ducked into the house. Two shots *pinged* past his head and he threw himself sideways into a pool of shadow.

A flight of stairs stretched to somewhere above—a ladder of darkness. Naughton fired at the top landing, and followed the slug as fast as his legs would carry him. As he pounded up the first flight, he caught the sound of running feet above.

The second flight of stairs carried him to a long corridor under the roof. As his head topped the landing he caught the outline of a man in an open doorway. A slug ripped the hat from Naughton's singed head and he dropped to his stomach, pushed his gun above the last step and fired twice. Then a door slammed, and he took a chance on raising his head.

He swung erect cautiously, moved with his shoulders sliding along the wall. Five paces from the closed door, he stopped. "Come out of there with your hands up!" he commanded.

Silence!

"If you find out who did it, kid, don't make no arrests!" Old Mac had told him.

Naughton's lips formed a bloodless line across his face.

"Come out, or I'm coming in after you!" He reiterated his command without moving those taut lips.

Three shots ploughed through the thin panel for an answer; three pellets of lead that missed him by inches. It was the answer he wanted.

HE PRESSED against the wall to gain momentum, fired twice at the lock, then catapulted ahead. His flying foot struck the lock, and the door crashed open, hanging crazily on broken hinges. He glimpsed a man crouched near the window and hurled himself sideways as a gun belched at him. Naughton squeezed the trigger... twice.

The first shot missed... the second was a dull click on an empty shell.

"I quit!" yelped the man, raising his hands. "My gun's empty!"

Naughton groped for a switch and flooded the room with light.

"I've got you, Rolph!" he rasped.

The insurance adjustor shrank before the detective's savagery. There was little of the debonair business man about him now as he swayed there, hands half raised.

Naughton talked, slowly, with the grim finality of a judge pronouncing sentence. "I've got you, Rolph, cold! I didn't suspect you, you rotten rat, but I should have. It was you who heard Clancy tell me that Torrence had talked, and so you sent those three bugs out to silence the girl. You had a swell spot, Rolph, hanging out at the MacGilray's where you could hear everything connected with departmental affairs. Perhaps when we come to it we'll find out you killed Manny and the Hansen girl."

"You can't prove a thing, Naughton. Give me a break. I can pay—"

"Pay!" yelled the detective. "You're going to pay right now. I'm going to take this gun and beat the life out of you. You've got you're break! Start fighting!"

Rolph suddenly whipped down his gun. Naughton realized he had been tricked, and sought to throw himself sideways. The other's gun exploded almost in his face. The slug tore into his shoulder, spun him around. He went down to one knee, shook his head to clear it and reversed his own revolver. Clutching it like a club, he came erect.

Rolph gaped, eyes distended in terror. In the weird, scorched face of the other man, he read a courage that cowed him and he retreated slowly.

"Don't, Naughton! I'll confess. I hired those bugs... Stay back. Don't stare at me like that! You're mad!"

Naughton laughed. His head spun dizzily. It was difficult to keep the weaving figure within the focus of his blurred vision, but he stalked doggedly, his whole consciousness centered on a single purpose.

And then—to his everlasting amazement—the man before him vanished, leaving the room filled with the echo of his scream!

Naughton stopped, bewildered. He shook his head savagely to dispel the blindness he was certain had descended on him. An understanding came to him as he staggered over to the shattered window casing. Shouts came filtering up from the street below. With a sigh of finality, Naughton turned and stumbled back to the stairs.

Captain Taylor met him at the door and helped him over to the squad-car where he collapsed in a weary heap on the running-board. From there he surveyed the scene. Nunnally was bent over a black mound on the sidewalk. For a moment Naughton thought that mound might represent young MacGilray, but the homicide dick walked over and disabused him.

"Rolph's finished," Nunnally growled. "Landed on his head."

Taylor touched the wounded shoulder. "You're hit, kid," he said gently.

Naughton pushed him aside so he could look around. "Where's Keith MacGilray? Is he—" He hesitated.

Taylor shook his head. "Pretty badly beaten up," he explained, "but nothing serious." He took a long breath, added: "I was afraid the kid had something to do with this arson mob; got a tip from the hospital that it was Keith that Ernie Torrence spotted at the Bilsky blaze. Afraid you were coverin' him, fella."

Naughton wagged his head. "No, it wasn't that. I just couldn't figure him. Well, you know Old Mac; a son of his couldn't—"

"How'd you spot Jack Rolph?"

THE ARSON dick shrugged wearily. "I wasn't absolutely sure until I went into that building after him. I only connected him when you were questioning me at the Hansen girl's apartment. It had to be him, though." He summarized the events leading up to the blow-off, explained wearily.

"Young Keith tried to make a case of his own; he wanted to succeed where we had failed, make a place for himself on the arson detail. Somehow he must have wormed his way into the mob without knowing—maybe he guessed it, though—that Rolph was back of it.

"The kid probably went into the Bilsky blaze to see if he couldn't snag a piece of evidence; he doesn't know fear around a fire. Torrence spotted him. Perhaps Ernie figured the kid was part of the mob, or maybe he realized the truth and wanted to tip me off to protect Keith from anything rash; we'll never be sure of that now. But that's what started things. Rolph was present when I was told that Torrence wanted to give me some information. The only way I can figure it is that he sent Wycoff's wife to block my car—he knew it well—while the bugs chased out to squelch Hansen. I dunno why they didn't bump her first, though."

"That checks," Taylor said quietly, "with the story Sarah Wycoff just delivered. She just belched out the whole thing, practically wrapped up for court. Only there ain't gonna be much need of a witness for Nunnally shot the hell out of Steve an' I got my doubts whether Ike'll ever be much good again either. We'll get Bilsky, though.

"But it went like you said. Rolph, of course, had a swell set-up. Him bein' an insurance adjustor, he was in a pretty spot. He started the fires, soaked the insurance companies all the traffic would stand, and took a big split from the insured. He knew what Keith was up to, but figured to use him while he could. When he heard about the Torrence episode, and then saw you workin' the kid over, he decided the thing had about run its course. He got the mob together an' they planned to do one more job an' have the pay-off.

"They let you hear them telephone young Keith on purpose. The plan was to kill him an' leave him on that warehouse job so's it would look like he was guilty of killin' the watchman. Torrence's incomplete statement would point to the idea that the kid was back of the Bilsky fire, an' both you an' the nurse would have to think the same thing when you heard Steve telephone the kid. Rolph also figured, so Sarah Wycoff tells us, that you'd be permanently out of the runnin' with this girl of Old Mac's.

"But Keith outsmarted them at the warehouse, an' so did you, by bein' there. They figured you two was dead, caught in the basement, but there was still the Hansen dame. Rolph hopped over there an' killed her. She must have delayed calling us. Maybe she was scared on account of what she'd done an' took too long to see the light. Then Rolph shot Manny rather than waste time trying to get those handcuffs off him. It just meant one less to split the take with. You broke up a bad mob, kid, an' I'm proud of you."

Naughton loosed a bitter laugh. "Me? Hell, it was the kid that—"

Taylor flagged him silent.

"All right, don't high-pressure me. We'll see that the kid gets all the breaks that's comin' to him; I'll even promise him a job on our detail when he's old enough. In the meantime, he's got one hell of a lot to learn about team-work, an' I can't figure anybody better suited for the job than one of his own family. So I figure about the best thing you can do is to hop over an' see this here gal of Old Mac's an' sort of get things started in the right direction. Nunnally an' me ain't so old we can't handle this cargo of cold meat."

Naughton chuckled again, but this time the bitterness was gone.

EYEWITNESS

HOMICIDE WORK'S NO BED OF ROSES UNDER ANY CONDITIONS, BUT WHEN NOT ONLY THE VICTIM, THE EVIDENCE, AND THE VERY SPOT WHERE THE BODY WAS FOUND ALL GO UP IN A PILLAR OF FLAME AFTER THE KILL IT CAN BECOME PLAIN HELL—AS TODD NAUGHTON LEARNED, WHEN HE WENT TO WORK ON THE CHARRED CORPSE IN THE CLOSET OF THE BURLINFORD DOG-TRACK.

CHAPTER ONE
THE CORPSE
IN THE CLOSET

WHEN THE blaze bored through the grandstand of the Burlinford Dog-Track it threw a hot scarlet splash against the midnight sky. It was visible for miles, and acted as a beacon to guide the third-alarm companies highballing from two directions.

Todd Naughton, central-office arson squad, glimpsed the tragically beautiful mirage as he whipped his red roadster out of the River Tube, and skidded along the main stem of the suburb, seconds ahead of the squawling ladder-truck of Company 17. With sirens sweeping the streets free of traffic they raced for the grounds, and when the arson dick caromed through the main gate of the dog-track, the big truck was so close behind it appeared to be shoving him with its powerful headlight beams.

NAUGHTON SKIDDED his roadster to a quick stop in a spot where it would be clear of the criss-crossed hose lines, silenced a shouting harness bull who wanted to object, and pushed through the police lines in search of the battalion chief in charge.

He found Chief Hardesly at the back of the roaring grandstand, face grimy and soot-streaked, in the center of the fight.

"Engine Eleven! Engine Eleven! Captain Doan! Your company lay a line to the track side of the fire. Lay it reverse to the hydrant at the south end of the stand. Hook the pumper in a line. Use a two-inch nozzle. Hurry it up! She won't last much longer!"

The hosemen of Engine 11 scurried to obey and Hardesly pushed off his helmet to wipe black sweat away. He saw Naughton, scowled, nodded in recognition.

The arson dick twisted him so he faced the mound on the ground.

"You don't get much evidence out of this blaze," he growled cynically. "We might as well all go home."

The hot flame sucked at them and the heat made the arson dick grimace. "Incendiary?" he asked.

Hardesly snorted, replaced his helmet. "What else! She broke out in three places at once. Kennels and at both ends of the stand. But there won't be anything standing to show that! I only hope I don't lose any men!"

Naughton frowned, spread a hand before his face to shield his eyes from the heat, and surveyed the scene. He knew the track—had attended the last big meet there. But it was an empty shell now; a total loss. Where once had stood the kennels were now steaming ashes. The track-rail was gone, and standing pathetically alone before the tottering grandstand was the white mechanical rabbit. His legs were stretched in mock speed, but he was now merely a twisted bit of metal that would delude the doggies no more. All this Naughton absorbed in one swift glance. It must have represented close to a hundred-thousand-dollar investment—fired deliberately, according to Hardesly!

A hoseman stumbled over, coughed smoke out of his lungs and said something to the battalion chief. Hardesly let out a string of oaths and pushed a blackened fist over his eyes. "Here's something for you to sink your teeth in, Naughton," he snarled, as three smoke-eaters staggered over bearing a limp burden in a canvas tarp. They dumped the thing in front of the chief. Almost automatically a white-clad interne appeared and jerked back the edge of the tarp.

It wasn't a pretty sight; even the interne winced. The clothing was burned away, save for the remnants of the shoes, and the flesh was roasted beyond all recognition. It was a charred ember with shoes on.

Hardesly instinctively moved around to protect the corpse from the flying spray with his broad body. "Where'd you find that?" he bellowed out, trying to make his voice carry above the thunder of the pumpers, the caterwauling of sirens, and the maniacal cackle of the flames.

"In a closet near the office," a hoseman answered hoarsely. "I was lookin' for a basement entrance—when I hacked away the door it tumbled out! The closet didn't go no place..." He panted to a stop, exchanged glances with one of his partners.

Another fireman clarified the accusation. "The door was locked on the outside! He must have been put in there—on purpose!"

"Back to your posts!" Hardesly ordered the hosemen.

Naughton stated at the thing that had once been human and sucked air through clenched teeth. A murder always tightened an investigation; made it doubly difficult to work out because the press clamored for immediate action. It brought in the homicide boys who wanted to clear up the cause of death, and not the source of the fire and those responsible.

NAUGHTON'S JOB was to find out who started the fires and secure evidence enough to convict. But arson isn't like murder or robbery; the fire itself is a confederate that destroys the evidence. In the case of a big blaze, touched off and planned by professional arsonists, there are no fingerprints, no weapon, and usually no witnesses. Fire is a robot that carefully removes all trace of the human wolves that gave it birth. Of the five-hundred-million-dollar annual national fire loss, over a hundred million is directly attributable to the arsonists.

As Naughton's eyes stayed fixed on the corpse, he thought of these things and an empty, nauseous ache formed in his stomach. The task was almost overwhelming.

He spoke to the interne. "Find anything, Doc?"

The white-uniformed man shrugged, wiping his hands. "Can't tell a damn thing without an autopsy—and what a sweet job that's going to be." He grimaced, and kicked the edge of the tarp over the charred mess.

Hardesly came over towing a frightened old man. "Here, Naughton, here's the watchman. Says he was asleep down by the kennels when the blaze broke out. Take a whiff an' you'll know why!" He pushed him over to the arson dick.

Naughton caught the aroma of alcohol that emanated from the scared watchman, a wispy little man of uncertain age who might have been fifty, or seventy. He had a drawn, horsy face that was seamed and gray-pallored, except for the nose which was criss-crossed purple against a scarlet background.

Naughton grabbed the man's arm to steady him, but it was evident that he was more scared than drunk. "What's your name?"

" 'Oward Watkins, sir," the watchman managed, with a noticeable cockney accent. "I hain't inebriated, sir, 'pon my word. I 'ad a bit of a nip, sir, that's all." He ogled Naughton hopefully through bulging, watery eyes that were blood-streaked. When he opened his mouth it looked as if some-one had removed every alternate tooth. Those which remained were yellow and odorous.

Naughton scowled. "What were you doing asleep? Aren't you likely to be fired for that?"

Watkins shrugged, "Mr. Quale, the gent what owns this 'ere plice, 'e's halready gimme me walkin' papers. So I just says to meself, I says, 'Oward, me lad, there hain't no percentage in you catchin' more cold, I says, so a bit of a nip of this 'ere gin will fix you up. I made me first round, sir, an' then I must 'ave taken a wee nap, for the next thing I knows, sir, one of them fire-laddies shikes me an' 'e says, ' 'Ere you, watcha doin' sleepin' when the 'owl plice is aflime!' 'E brings me over 'ere, an' 'ere I am, sir."

Naughton's eyes narrowed perceptibly. "Quale fired you, but didn't put another watchman in your place?"

" 'E didn't hexactly fire me, sir. 'E just says, ' 'Oward, old friend, you might as well look for another job. This 'ere plice is gonna close up in a few diys.' "

"Did he say why it was going to close?"

Watkins licked his lips and looked from Hardesly to Naughton, " 'E didn't siy, sir!"

The arson dick took Watkins' arm, twisted him around so he was facing the covered mound on the ground, then removed the tarp. "Anything familiar about that?" he demanded, eyeing the little cockney.

Watkins jackknifed as though kicked in the stomach. "Ow, my God!" he moaned, his horse face lengthening. He clung to Naughton with a taloned paw and went sick.

The detective kicked the covering over the corpse, took tire gagging watchman by the arm and led him behind the police lines to his roadster. Hardesly paused just long enough to turn the command over to a subordinate and hurried after them.

NAUGHTON PUSHED Watkins onto the running-board of the official car and gave him time to recover somewhat. The little cockney gripped a scrawny knee in each bony hand to keep them from trembling. His protruding eyes were focused rigidly on the ground as though they still retained the image which had startled them,

"Recognize it?" Naughton asked finally.

Watkins shook his head. "Gor blime me, mister, I bloody well couldn't! Ow my God!"

"Pull yourself together, Watkins!" Naughton growled. "Who else was on the grounds when you took your—little nip?"

"Nobody, s'elp me. I cime on duty early, an' made a bit of chinge on the last race. I was feelin' pretty good, sir. I give old Joe, the beggar, a dollar—the big gamblers all do that for luck, sir, for old Joe, 'e's blind, you unnerstan'—an' I drop by the office to check in an' siy 'ello to Mr. Quale an' Mr. Bermet, 'is bookkeeper.

"The crowd 'ad left shortly after twelve. Then the 'andlers an' the bookie 'ung around another 'arf hour but them, too, was all gone by one o'clock, sir."

"And then you took your bit of a nap, eh?" Hardesly put in sourly.

"I mide sure the gite was locked, sir!" Watkins retorted.

"Who could that dead guy be?"

Watkins shuddered. "I'm sure I down't know! 'E wasn't supposed to be 'ere after closin' time!"

Naughton sniffed. "From the way be was found, he was apparently supposed to be there for some time. It couldn't be Quale?"

Hardesly vetoed that suggestion. "It isn't Maurice Quale, One of my boys talked to him on the phone a little while ago. He's on his way over now."

"Know anything about the insurance on the place, Watkins? Remember, I can check up later."

The watchman looked scared. "You think miybe some'un done it deliberate?"

"Answer my question," Naughton snapped. "What kind of insurance did Maurice Quale have on this track?"

"Suppose you ask me that question?" a voice asked abruptly.

Naughton swung slowly around to face the newcomer who had joined them. He surmised the stranger was Quale even before Watkins plaintively corroborated it.

"I done the best I could, sir," the watchman babbled. "I hain't responsible for it, sir, s'elp me God, Mr. Quale."

The arson dick sized up his man. This Quale was a big fellow, close-knit, panther-lithe. The lurid flame-light splashed red across a face that was long, woodeny; the eyes were palely devoid of expression. Quale looked hard, capable, cool. Despite the dramatic tension of the meeting, the nerve-racking excitement of the fire, he seemed as calm and collected as though he faced two casual acquaintances in a hotel lobby.

Naughton nodded, as though in approval. "I'm Naughton of the arson squad," he introduced himself. "Is this layout a one-man institution?"

"I own it—yes," Quale acknowledged.

"Insured?"

The track-owner stiffened slightly. His features remained wooden, but the whole face seemed to darken as he met Naughton's quizzical stare. "For fifty thousand. And if you think I had anything to do with this fire, you're crazy! In spite of the insurance, I stand to lose about thirty thousand besides, to say nothing of a greyhound worth—"

Watkins interrupted. "You didn't lose *Battle-Cry*, Mister Quale! Miss Nina took 'im away after the last rice, sir, an' I'm-sure—" He smothered his words with a hand hastily thrown over his mouth as though he had said too much.

Quale stabbed the watchman with piercing, expressionless eyes. "Of course, I remember now. Thank you, Watkins for correcting me." Watkins winced as though struck, and Quale turned back to Naughton.

"As you probably know, Nina is my daughter. *Battle-Cry* is her dog. He won the second race tonight and we decided to withdraw him for the season."

NAUGHTON FELT a surge of elation. He was beginning to get somewhere now. One of the elementary moves in an arson investigation is to find out if the insured has removed anything of sentimental value from the premises just prior to the fire. Nina Quale had removed the pet grey-hound from the doomed track just after the last race. That was a significant fact, and Naughton was satisfied in his own mind that Quale had lied when he stated that he was aware of his daughter's action. He tried a new tack.

"The firemen found a body," he announced quietly, watching the track-owner's face. "Locked in a closet near your office."

That jolted the other man. "Who…?" Quale half-turned toward the watchman as though expecting the answer would come from that source.

"Watkins couldn't identify the body," Naughton cut in. "It was badly burned. Have you any ideas?"

"You said it was *locked* in the closet?"

Naughton bobbed his head. "Locked!"

Quale turned slowly to Watkins. "Did Mr. Bennet return after he left with me?"

Watkins shook his head decisively. "'E never did, Mr. Quale."

Quale took a step close to his watchman. The flickering flame-light on his face gave it a saturnine cast. "You've been drinking, Watkins!" he said coldly. "Where'd you get it?"

The cockney's eyes popped and he licked his parched lips. "Hit was a gift, sir."

"From whom?"

The watchman was obviously scared—plenty scared. Naughton was puzzled, so he did not interfere. Quale reached out a big hand that closed like a bear-trap on the shoulders of the little Limey. Watkins whimpered, went limp with fear.

"Who gave you that gin?" Quale asked very low.

Watkins moved his jaw several times before the words came; like water from a freshly primed hand-pump. "Mr. Poole, sir!" he managed finally.

Quale released his grip so suddenly that Watkins dropped to the ground. The track-owner's face relaxed into that curiously immobile mask; it seemed as if both mind and feeling had abandoned the man's body. Quale moved and spoke like an automaton.

"I have a suite at the Haycox Hotel," he told the arson dick. "You can find me there if you have any further questions." With that remark, he swung on his heel and strode stiffly away.

Watkins gave a strangled sob and massaged his shoulder where the track-owner's hand had gripped him. " 'E's a 'ard man, a very 'ard man," he whined. " 'Ave you gent'men done with me?"

Naughton watched the retreating figure of Quale until it had vanished into the crowd, then turned slowly to the cringing watchman.

"I told you the God's truth!" mumbled the cockney.

Naughton fished a small whistle from his vest pocket, blew it once. A moment later a big harness bull hurried over.

"You whistle?"

Naughton displayed his own badge. "Take this little rat downtown and lock him up. Book him to me as a material witness," he instructed.

Watkins squirmed, but the big cop collared him. "Gor blime this is a houtrige!" he gasped. "I hain't a common criminal!"

Naughton sniffed. "I want you where I can find you. You haven't told all you know. Think it over."

Watkins was prone to argue the point but a roar from the fire lines drowned his words. The grandstand was folding up! Hardesly spat an oath and started to run. Naughton paused long enough to see the cop drag Watkins away, then he followed the chief as the back of the grandstand broke!

The blaze let out a defiant roar, spraying flaming cinders in a fountain of fire. A panting pumper thundered to safety. Hosemen tugged fiercely on their lines. The roof buckled, began to fall forward. The mechanical rabbit vanished beneath several tons of debris.

Hardesly made a hurried check to see that his men were all clear, then he took off his helmet, wiped the sweat hand and heaved a long sigh. "Well," he said wearily, "that just about finishes my work, Naughton."

"Mine's just beginning!" growled the arson dick.

CHAPTER TWO
50 — 40:10

AS NAUGHTON expected, the discovery of the corpse brought in the homicide squad and when, at three o'clock in the morning, he tooled his red roadster to a stop in front of the morgue, he saw the big squad car. He offered up a half-prayer and pushed into the grim building.

He found Sergeant Kane and another homicide dick named Kovack in the office of Doctor Phillips, the autopsy surgeon. The surgeon had just finished reading his report to the two homicide detectives, and he summarized it briefly for Naughton.

"From the bone structure," Phillips told them, "I presume the deceased was a man about fifty or fifty-five. He was shot in the chest three times from a small-calibered pistol—I should say a twenty-five automatic. However, in my opinion, he was not dead when the fire started."

"The killer let him have three slugs and then chucked him in the closet to die," Kane summed up. "That it, Doc?"

"Briefly," Phillips admitted, "that's about it."

Naughton leaned against the opposite corner of the desk and looked at the two central-office men. The sergeant was chunky, with a long trunk and short, sturdy legs. In profile, he looked fat, soft, but that was just an illusion he fostered. He was hard inside and out. He was a good dick, and he made up in honesty what he lacked in tact and culture. His callous indifference to death and tragedy jolted the young arson dick; but Kane had worked homicides for twelve years and knew enough to fortify himself against any emotionalism he might have.

Kovack was a tall, silent Pole. His face was a mask that never changed. He seldom spoke and when he did it was merely a tardy echo of something Kane had said earlier. They were able to work together for the simple reason that Kovack did as he was told, offered no suggestions and agreed with the aggressive sergeant. Sergeant Kane did not like to be crossed, blocked or interfered with in his work; he wanted to do the thinking. For that reason alone Naughton hated to get on the same case with the irascible veteran.

Not that he didn't respect Kane—he did, up to a certain point. Kane had been out of uniform fifteen years; Naughton had been out only one. But he had made good in his new post, even if old veterans like Kane refused to acknowledge that Naughton had won his spurs after only two years in uniform. He hadn't served enough time in harness, they said.

Now Kane surveyed him with good-natured tolerance. "Well, kid, did you find out who the stiff is?"

Naughton gave a wry grin. "I'm afraid not, Sergeant."

"Well," chuckled Kane. "Just what did you find out?"

Naughton detailed his talk with Watkins and Quale; he put emphasis on the watchman's statement that Nina Quale had taken the greyhound, *Battle-Cry*, out of the kennels just before they were destroyed by the fire. He told how agitated Quale had appeared when he had learned of his daughter's action, and how ferociously the track-owner had pressed Watkins regarding the gift of gin.

KANE LISTENED in silence. As Naughton talked, thre sergeant reamed out the bowl of an odorous briar with the broken blade of a pen knife. Kovack leaned in a corner, his eyes focused on infinity. When the arson dick concluded his resumé, Kane smacked the pipe against his palm, dumped the dottle on the floor and looked up.

"That watchman knows more than he told you, kid," he commented.

"That's what I think," Naughton admitted. "I'd like to know more about the Poole angle. Suppose he means Guy Poole, the gambler, eh?"

"Sure. Poole's a rat. He used to run a saloon when I tramped a beat in the old Fifth Ward. But you don't need to worry none about Poole, son. Old Kovack an' me'll knock off this case just one, two, three. How about it, you dumb Pollack?"

Kovack nodded somberly, "Sure, Sarge, we'll knock it off like you say. One, two, three."

"That one, two, three stuff sounds as if you're getting ready to jump someplace," Naughton grinned.

"We are," Kane assured him tartly. "First we'll jump over and grab a plate of ham-and-eggs. Every time Kovack an' me come to the morgue we like to eat ham-and-eggs right away afterwards. Don't we, Kovy?"

"Every time," the poker-faced dick agreed. "The Sarge always eats ham-'n-eggs after we come to the morgue."

Kane went on: "Then we'll jump right over to the can an' take this gin-drinking Limey apart. I'll show you how to make him talk." He thrust the pipe into his pocket, tilted his hat at a belligerent angle and stood squarely on his feet.

"S'long, Doc, sorry you can't join us in some eggs-and-ham. Come on, Naughton."

The arson dick grimaced but followed the tug-boat figure of the sergeant. Kovack trailed along as though he were in tow.

Outside it was decided that Naughton would drive his own car to headquarters and meet Kane and his partner at the tiny lunch-counter across the street from the jail. He stood at the curb and watched Kovack swing the squad car into motion. The Pollack could drive, even if he couldn't talk.

As the homicide wagon rolled out of sight, Naughton walked over to his roadster and slid under the wheel. He felt depressed. Kane was taking the case out of his hands, yet there seemed nothing he could do about it. He fished a cigarette from his pocket, lighted it and reached for the ignition key. Perhaps another talk with Watkins would turn up something concrete.

Abruptly a figure loomed out of the shadow and glided to the edge of the car. There was something so furtive in the man's movements that Naughton instinctively readied for his service revolver. But there was no need for a gun.

"Don't be noivous, pal, don't be noivous," soothed the newcomer in a husky, confidential whisper. "Ain't you the flatty what works the fires?"

Naughton slowly withdrew his hand from the butt of his gun. "I'm with the arson squad," he admitted. "Who are you?" He leaned forward to glimpse the face of the other.

The stranger was fox-featured with narrow, oblique eyes and a mouth that twitched constantly from some nervous ailment. He wore a foppish brown-toned derby, a collar that was patently celluloid and a garish checkered suit. The man definitely smacked of the race-tracks.

"It don't make no difference to you who I am, pal," the other suggested in that same hushed, ingratiating tone. "It's what I know, now ain't it?"

Naughton took a long, slow breath. Here was a typical informer; paradoxically, an invaluable rat.

"Well, what do you know?"

The fox-faced stranger gave a low, nasty chuckle. "What I know depends on what you can pay," he went on, and when he saw Naughton's features darken belligerently, added: "Easy, pal, easy. You can't get no place with that rough stuff—not with me, you can't. When I get something, I sees my mouthpiece. If he says I can collect—I can collect."

TODD NAUGHTON submerged the impulse to spring out of the car and administer a pistol-whipping to the informer. But a smart copper plays his angles; one tip from a rat like this can save you weeks and even months of perhaps futile work. He pushed open the door of the road-ster.

"Climb in. We'll talk this over."

The other man grinned slyly, shook his head and shut the door. Then he leaned his elbows on the top and stuck his head into the interior. "I'll take mine standin'," he leered. "But I seen you come out of there with those other flatfeet, and then sit in this here wagon like you wished you knew something about the fire at the Burlinford Track."

Naughton ran his tongue around the inside of his mouth. "The police department can't put out any dough," he said slowly, feeling his way. "But if you've got something that will prove arson, the insurance companies might be grate-ful. That's the only thing I can do for you."

The man with the fox-face thought that one over. "Suppose," he began finally, "just supposing now—I could tip you off to the reason the fire was started, that it was something to do with the insurance...." He riveted his slit eyes on the detective's face.

"That ought to result in some dough for you," Naughton admitted.

"I'd have to tell you who I am," the fellow hesitated.

"The police always protect the identity of an informer," Naughton now told him frankly. "If they failed to, they'd get no more tips. You've got to trust them because you can't get paid until your information is checked. We don't even record the name of an informer in our report."

The stranger hesitated but a moment longer, then he tugged open the door and climbed inside. "You got an honest face," he offered. "I guess I can trust you. Just keep drivin' this buggy around. It don't do my rep no good to be seen parked with a flatty. You get me, pal, don't you?"

Naughton started the motor, let the roadster glide into motion. "Spill it in a lump," he advised. "I'm due at head-quarters in a few minutes. Let's start with your name."

"Jobelman," announced the informer. "The boys call me Nifty—Nifty Jobelman. I run a little book—oh, well, here and there, if you get me, pal."

"All right, Nifty. Who started that blaze?"

Jobelman chuckled, then continued in his oily whisper. "Now I didn't see nobody start no fire, get that, pal. But I ain't dumb. Now I'll give you the numbers an' you add 'em. Ready, pal? Well, that little playground for the doggies an' the hoi-polloi set a certain gent back about a hundred G's."

"Maurice Quale?"

"Who else, pal! All right. Now Brother Quale gets himself involved in a little deal which didn't pan out so hot so he winds up holding the sack an' a very tough gent named Poole holds his note for forty G's. Still with me, pal? Okie. So this tough gent—"

"Guy Poole?" hazarded Naughton.

JOBELMAN GAVE a brittle snicker. "I hate to mention the names of very tough gents, especially when they got a lot of tougher pals, but between me an' you an' this red buggy—the answer is yes. Like I says, this tough gent holds a note for forty G's and wants a track that's worth a hundred G's. The owner is stymied, till he remem-bers that the track is insured for fifty G's. Now, pal, forty from fifty leaves ten, an' a guy can put a lot of distance between himself an' very tough guys on ten G's. It ain't a hundred G's, mind you, but it's better than a kick in the face."

Naughton turned the roadster into the park and cut his speed. "You mean that Quale owed Poole forty thousand

and rather than lose the track for that amount, he burned it for the insurance. Then he'll pay off the forty thousand and still have the remaining ten. Right?"

"Your arithmetic is poifect," Nifty Tobelman chortled. "An' now when do I collect?"

Naughton skipped that one. "What about that corpse, Nifty? Who was it?"

Jobelman made a patting motion with his right hand. "Nix, pal, nix. I don't want to get mixed up with them tough homicide flattys. I ain't got any ideas who the stiff was, an' I don't want any. In fact, pal, I don't want to talk about it."

"What were you doing at the morgue?"

The informer hesitated. "I seen you talkin' to the smoke-eater in the white slicker. Then I missed you, an' I asked white-coat where you'd gone. He says to the morgue, most likely, so I grabs a cab."

"Did you see Nina Quale at the track tonight?"

Jobelman started, seemed surprised. "So what?"

"I'm asking you," Naughton growled.

Jobelman shook his head hastily. "Pal, I gave you my load for the night. You don't get any more goods until you pay for this."

Naughton knew better than to press his advantage. "O.K., Nifty. I'll look into it. If there's anything to your story, I'm sure I can get some ducats for you from the insurance company. Where can I reach you?"

Nifty Jobelman hesitated a long time. "Call the Acme Sporting Palace," he said finally, "an' ask for Sam an' leave a private number where I can call you. Lay off the official stuff, pal. I'll buzz you within thirty minutes at the most. Now lemme out at the foist taxi-stand."

CHAPTER THREE
MURDER MISS

WHEN NAUGHTON was rid of the informer, he high-balled to headquarters. Now he felt, he was getting some place! If Jobelman's story were correct, then Quale was his man. Nina Quale must have known the place was doomed—why else would she remove the greyhound?

Here was motive! Quale's original alibi that the track was insured for a little over half its value was shattered by the story of Jobelman. A jury would regard the evidence of straightened circumstances as sufficient to prompt the owner to attempt "quick sale" of his property to some insurance company.

Quale might have an alibi for the time the fire actually started, bat Naughton was sure he could offset that. Quale could have arranged a fuse—perhaps the old candle trick— affording him a couple of hours grace before the fire actually broke out. Battalion Chief Hardesly's testimony that the blaze started in three places at once would help to discredit Quale.

The only fly in the ointment was that bottle of gin. Why, Naughton demanded of himself, should Guy Poole give old Watkins a bottle of gin, and why, too, should Quale become so agitated about it?

He was still grappling unsuccessfully with that problem when he rolled up in front of police headquarters. He walked across the street, glanced through the window of Petie's Dining Car, but Kane and Kovack were nowhere in sight. He retraced his steps and met the two homicide dicks tramping out of the station-house.

Kane was scowling. "A hell of a smart dick you turned out to be!" he growled at Naughton. "Juggin' a valuable witness in the main jail!"

Naughton paused. "Meaning—just what?"

"Meanin'," Kane snarled, "that you should have locked him up in some suburban jug where they couldn't get at him!"

Naughton stiffened. "You mean he wouldn't talk to you?"

"I'll say he wouldn't," the sergeant bit savagely. "For the simple reason a shyster lawyer walked in here with a writ and a few bucks and sprung him while we was at the morgue. He's probably on a boat to China by this time."

Naughton frowned, then started to grin. With the dope Jobelman had given him, they might be able to get along without the little cockney. He was about to confide in the sergeant, when the latter's next explosion silenced him.

"That's the trouble with puttin' you damn kids into plainclothes before you know anythin' about police work! Come on, Kovy, let's get goin'." He brushed past Naughton and climbed into the squad car.

Kovack regarded Naughton blankly for a minute, then slid under the wheel.

"You can both go to hell!" Todd Naughton flung at the moving car. Soured, be pushed off home and went to bed,

AS HE expected, the insurance company started to squawk. Naughton woke to the jangle of the telephone. It was Logan, special agent for the State Mutual. Logan's company had issued the policy on the Burlinford Track, and knowing the blaze was incendiary, wanted some action before issuing a check. Naughton agreed to meet Logan uptown at noon and hung up. It was ten now.

The arson dick climbed out of his crumpled pajamas and took a needle-beating from a cold shower. After that he felt better, inside and out.

He left his apartment by a quarter to eleven. Too early to meet Logan, and he wasn't hungry enough to eat. Drink? That reminded him....

He called a friend on the vice squad and found that Guy Poole maintained a suite on the ninth floor of the Grant Hotel. Naughton walked to the garage, wheeled out his little red buggy and drove over.

He didn't bother with the desk but went directly to the elevator and was whisked aloft to the ninth. The floor-clerk was a little snooty; he insisted that it was a standing order of Mr. Poole's that he wasn't to be disturbed before noon, not even, the nattily groomed young man insisted, if the hotel were on fire.

Naughton took out his buzzer and bounced it once on the desk.

"I'll do the disturbing," he informed the now startled clerk. "Either you give me the suite-number or I'll start kicking in doors until I get the right one."

The clerk acted as though he were betraying his own mother when he finally admitted that Mr. Poole's suite was Number 938.

Naughton walked down the corridor until he found the right door, knocked, waited. After a pause the door was opened by a flat-shouldered giant without a neck.

"I want to see Guy Poole," Naughton told him, adding, "And I don't want an argument, Jumbo. Hop along, now."

The big man cocked his head like a rooster surveying a worm. "Mr. Poole," he announced huskily, "ain't in."

"In or up," Naughton snapped. "I see him."

The big man's chest started to swell. He turned sideways like a fighter moving into his stance.

"It don't pay," Naughton warned him grimly, "to get tough with a copper."

While the big fellow was digesting that, a second man strolled into view. This man was slight, with silver-toned hair brushed smooth off a sloping forehead. His rosy cheeks suggested many prolonged sessions in barbers' chairs. He wore pajamas, open at the neck, and a brocaded silk lounging-robe. He looked at Naughton with lazy gray eyes that were singularly devoid of expression. "What's the argument, Benny?" he drawled.

"This copper," Benny muttered, "was tryin' to make a monkey outta me."

"Copper?"

"If you're Guy Poole," Naughton told the silver-thatched man, "I want a word with you."

At Poole's nod, Benny moved aside for Naughton to enter, then closed the door.

The suite—what Naughton could see of it—was spacious and ultra-modern. There was a radio-bar standing under a huge, frameless mirror. Benny moved lumberingly toward this and waited.

"Drink?" Poole asked, and when Naughton shook his head, waved the square-hulled man out of the room. He gestured casually in the direction of some chairs and dropped into the nearest one himself, without waiting to see whether the arson dick was going to sit or stand.

NAUGHTON MEASURED Poole. This guy was wise; it would be a waste of time trying to trick or trap him into an admission. A blunder like that would probably result in the hurried visit of a shyster lawyer and then he never would get a word out of the gambler.

"You're Naughton of the arson detail, I believe," Poole observed languidly.

Naughton gave a wry grin. How in hell did Poole know who he was? "That's right," he admitted. "I suppose you know the greyhound track went up in smoke."

Poole nodded indifferently. "Too bad. Nice lay-out. I was there last night. As a matter of fact, I feel a little guilty." The gambler chuckled ruefully. "One of the boys gave me a bottle of gin. I never touch the stuff, so I gave it to the old cockney watchman. They tell me he was so drunk the firemen had trouble waking him up."

Naughton almost gasped aloud. He felt like an actor whose lines have been stolen. He had anticipated a long argument to wheedle that admission out of Guy Poole, and now the gambler had simply dumped it into his lap, and by so doing had nullified its value.

"You hold a note of Maurice Quale's?" Naughton queried.

Poole's smile was enigmatic. "You know, Naughton, in my business we just don't discuss personal matters, such as loans, notes, winnings you know what I mean."

"We do in my business," the detective came back. "I happen to know that Maurice Quale owes you forty thousand dollars!"

Poole yawned, pried open a glass cigarette case with slender fingers and forked a smoke. "A lot of people owe me money," he remarked. "Sometimes I get it, and again, sometimes I don't." He smiled. "And by the way, Naughton, I never keep books. That tip might save you a little work."

Naughton said: "Thanks—it might. Has this note of Quale's any connection with the fact that you bailed

Howard Watkins out of jail early this morning and spirited him away?" It was a blind shot.

Poole's mouth twisted into a sardonic grin. He looked down at the cigarette, rolling it with his index finger and thumb to loosen the tobacco. His gray eyes were inscrutable. "You'll have to hit me again," he told Naughton. "I didn't draw anything in that hand."

"Where is Watkins, Poole?"

"How should I know? Because I give a bum a bottle of bad gin is no sign I sit up nights keeping tabs on him. Act your age, copper!"

Naughton knew they had reached an impasse. It was nearly twelve, anyhow, and he had promised to meet Logan at the Hole-in-the-Wall. He got up, started for the door. Halfway to it, he paused, turned slowly. Poole had remained seated and surveyed him through lazy eyes.

"You may get a call from the homicide squad," Naughton suggested. "There was a dead guy found in a closet near the office. Have you any idea who he might have been?"

Poole smiled thinly. "I'll call you if I get any ideas."

Naughton felt his ears grow red. Stymied! By a heel, too! He turned toward the door leading into the corridor when it burst open abruptly and the broad back of the gigantic Benny lurched foremost into the room. Naughton took a long step sideways, got behind a tall grandfather's clock. In the big mirror over the radio-bar, he saw the girl.

She was crowding Benny ahead of her, a small blued-steel revolver menacing his stomach. As she cleared the door and got into the room, she heeled the panel shut and jerked sideways so that the muzzle of her little gun took in Guy Poole.

The gambler was still seated, but he had skewed forward until he was perched on the edge of the chair. The cigarette hung cold from straight lips.

THE GIRL herself was young—Naughton's quick estimate placed her at twenty-five. She was dark with brown eyes that should have been large, but were now crow-footed into narrow slits. Her slim figure was encased in a smartly tailored suit, and she wore flat-heeled oxfords.

"All right, Mr. Poole!" she rasped. "You wanted trouble, so here it is...."

Naughton knocked her wrist up as the gun went off. The slug struck the rounded edge of the ceiling and sprinkled plaster so that it settled like dandruff on the silk shoulders of Poole's dressing gown.

The arson dick yanked the gun out of her fingers with his left hand; with his right he caught her shoulder and sprawled her into a chair. She said, "Oh, damn!" when he first grabbed her. After that she said nothing.

Poole lifted himself out of the chair, leaned five fingers on the table nearby. Big Benny started to whine. "Geez, chief! I didn't see the gun—not at first. She says, 'This is Mr. Poole's apartment?' and when I start to tell her you're busy, she pushes this heater into my belly—"

"Shut up, Benny!" Poole said wearily. "This calls for a drink all around."

Naughton looked down at the girl. "Lucky I was handy," he told her sourly.

She looked him straight in the eye. "Not for me it wasn't!" she snapped, then added, "You heel!"

Naughton glanced over his shoulder at Poole. The gambler accepted a long drink from the quavering hand of Benny, raised his own in a mock salute.

The dick shook his head disgustedly. "She thinks I'm connected with you, Poole," he growled. "If you want to prefer charges, I'll take her along."

The girl shot a quick, suspicious glance at the detective. Poole continued to smile. It was a hard, meaningless expression with neither mirth nor warmth. "The next time you intend to shoot anyone, my dear Nina," he leered over his glass, "don't do it with a policeman in the room."

Naughton squinted hard at the girl. "Nina...? Are you Nina Quale?"

She was staring at him, puzzled. "A policeman? And I missed! Damn!"

"Let her go, Naughton," Poole said. "She wasn't trying to hit anyone. She was simply trying to show me the gun and it went off. An accident."

Nina Quale rose unsteadily. "It was an accident that I missed you, you rotten rat!"

"Forget it, kid," Poole told her. "You'll talk yourself into trouble. This copper's hungry for somebody to work on. That's why he's here."

Naughton gave a thin smile. He hefted the girl's gun, dropped it into his hip pocket then took her arm. "Come on, Nina. We'll grab a little fresh air."

"S'long," Poole called cheerfully. "Sorry I couldn't help— either of you."

"I'll be seein' you," Naughton threw at him softly.

The girl said nothing on the way down. Naughton retained his hold on her arm, steered her out the side entrance onto Hall Street. Stopped.

"Now, Nina, what's this all about?"

She held his eyes with hers. "Am I under arrest?"

Naughton shook his head. "No, but I'd like to ask you a few questions."

She freed her arm. "I have no information that would possibly be of interest to you," she said shortly. "It is strictly my own business." She swung on her heel, walked to the corner and climbed into a cab.

Naughton watched the taxi melt into the noon stream of traffic, then tramped the half-block to his own roadster.

CHAPTER FOUR

BATTLE-CRY

LOGAN WAS already at the Hole-in-the-Wall, holding a table. After they had given their orders, he asked the arson dick what he had.

Naughton went over his case, watching the insurance operative—a slim, trim youngster—as he talked.

When he concluded, Logan said: "No matter which way you look at it, it's got to be Quale. We've got a beautiful set-up for motive. I understand the track's been losing money steadily."

"I've been out once or twice in the last month. They had a pretty fair crowd every time."

Logan shrugged. "Well, we'll see. I've made an appointment with Simon Bennet, Quale's bookkeeper and office man."

"Will he talk?"

Logan smiled. "That's why I made the date for after lunch, Naughton. You've got more weight than I have on that sort of thing. They say this old fellow's a pretty easy-going egg; shouldn't have too much trouble."

Naughton brought up the subject of the informer's pay. The insurance man frowned. "That's one thing I hate to sanction," he admitted. "But we have a fund for the purpose. From your story, it looks as though this informer had the real inside on Quale and his dealings with Poole."

They finished the lunch, paid off and went outside. The trip to the bookkeeper's was made in Naughton's red roadster.

BENNET LIVED in a small, obscure, apartment hotel. He had a suite which consisted, so far as Naughton could make but, of three rooms—bedroom, living-room and bath. It was cheaply furnished, but comfortable enough.

Bennet was alone. He was about fifty-five or thereabouts. He was nearsighted with thick-lensed glasses and a habit of squinting over the top of them. Even judicious combing had failed to cover his pate with graying hair. His cheeks were hollow, his shoulders stooped from years of desk-work. He greeted the two investigators amiably enough.

Naughton drove right to his point. "You keep the books and handle the office affairs for Maurice Quale. Is that right?"

Bennet nodded. He carefully adjusted his glasses on his nose. "I did most of the clerical work for the track, yes." His voice was gentle, but it trembled slightly.

"How much money had the track lost in the last season," Naughton wanted to know.

Bennet looked from one to the other. He wagged his head. "I can't carry figures in my head."

Logan frowned. "What you mean is—you won't tell us. Is that it, Bennet?"

The older man toyed with a watch-chain. "Gentlemen, Mr. Quale was mighty decent to me. If he's in a jam the only thing I can do is to demonstrate my loyalty by keeping my mouth shut. I've always been a law-abiding citizen; never in my entire life, which, gentlemen, covers more years than either of you have seen, have I refused to assist the authorities whenever possible. Not until now. I'm sorry, but all the books and records of the Quale track were destroyed in the fire. I remember nothing about them."

Naughton lighted a cigarette, regarded it thoughtfully. "You're not helping Quale by your attitude, Bennet. Any jury in the world would regard your action as prejudicial to the best interests of Maurice Quale. Instead of helping, you're hurting him."

Bennet gave them a tired smile. "I wouldn't hurt Maurice Quale for the world. Nor can you trick me into telling you any more than I already have. My frank statement, gentlemen, is that I have no recollection of the condition of those books."

Logan said: "Mind if I use your phone, Mr. Bennet?"

Bennet shook his head, indicated the instrument half hidden in a wall niche.

"Help yourself."

Logan called his office, asked for any calls and said he was coming in. Then he hung up and nodded his head toward the phone. "Sergeant Kane's been trying to locate you, Naughton. Called my office. Perhaps he's found something. Better call him."

Naughton ground out his cigarette, called headquarters, and was connected with the homicide.

Kane's voice was almost savage. "I've got your witness, Naughton. The Limey."

Naughton said: "Swell, Sarge. Where is he?"

Kane laughed, nastily. "In the morgue with the top of his head perforated. We picked him out of a new sewer trench on the North Side near the city limits. Just thought you'd like to know." He hung up.

Naughton pronged the receiver, kept his hand on it.

"Bad news?" Logan asked.

"Watkins, the track watchman, got himself killed."

Bennet chimed in: "Not the little Englishman?" At the detective's nod, he went on, "Oh, say, I'm mighty sorry to hear that! Poor devil! Do they know who did it?"

"The sergeant didn't say." Naughton's tone became harder. "Now, listen to me, Bennet, there's something screwy about this case. We've got two killings so far—there may be more. Either you talk, or we'll take you in for concealing vital evidence."

Bennet's face went a flat white. "I'm afraid you are attaching too much importance to what I know," he faltered, after a long pause. "Frankly, gentlemen, the track *has* lost money this last season, but surely you can't imply from that that Maurice Quale would—"

"How much money did it lose?" Logan put in.

"About thirty thousand—roughly."

"And the season's about over?"

Bennet shrugged. "There were to be two more races."

Naughton asked: "What about *Battle-Cry?* How'd he do?"

The old bookkeeper gave him a side-wise look. "*Battle-Cry* did pretty well for his owners. Miss Quale had several tempting offers for him of late."

"Did Guy Poole want to purchase him?"

Bennet looked surprised. "Why! Why, I think there was something said about it—about Mr. Poole wanting him."

"I understand that Poole holds a note of Mr. Quale's?"

The old man's face hardened. "I won't discuss that!" he snapped.

Naughton eased up. "By the way, do you know a bookie by the name of Nifty Jobelman?"

Simon Bennet hesitated, then smiled ruefully. "I think I know who you mean. He usually wears a brown derby. I could hardly confess to actually knowing him, although I know who you mean. Why did you ask?"

"I wanted to know," Naughton told him shortly.

THE TWO dicks went out. Going through the lobby, Naughton said half to himself: "I'd like to know where that dog is."

Logan shrugged. "Why worry about a damned dog. This practically cinches the case against Quale."

"I can't arrest him on what we've got," Naughton argued.

"That's your worry. I'm going to advise the company to refuse to pay the policy check. We've got enough to make that stick in a civil court even if you can't do it in a criminal action."

"There are two dead guys in this ease," Naughton growled, "and that means a killer is loose. Maybe Maurice Quale killed them, and maybe he didn't. There's got to be a criminal action started somewhere."

"Then you worry about it."

The arson dick nodded. "That's what I'm doing, Logan. I want you to recommend that your company pay off— today."

"You must be nuts!" snapped the insurance op.

"I'm not nuts. Quale couldn't have handled a job like that by himself; he had to have help."

"What about that daughter of his. She's tough enough, from your own story, to set fire to a building. A dame that would attempt to kill a man would burn a racetrack."

"A lot of people wouldn't regard the killing of Guy Poole as murder. She's not so tough, or she wouldn't have risked putting herself and her father into a spot by sneaking her dog out—not if she was in on the fire."

"Maybe she didn't know it would be uncovered. Perhaps she threw the slug into old Watkins so he wouldn't be able to testify against her."

"I thought of that, too," Naughton admitted. "But you can tell a lot from just meeting people. Now I don't think she did it."

"So, because you like the way a gal holds her gun, you want my company to pay her old man fifty grand? Listen, Naughton, I'm worried about you."

They reached the arson dick's roadster. Naughton opened the door, slid under the wheel and motioned Logan to climb into the seat beside him. Then he picked up the strings of his argument.

"We can blow up this case if you'll pay the fifty grand."

Logan grinned sardonically. "Sure, and what happens to the fifty G's? Quale pays off Poole and we lose the dough, or else he takes the whole thing and blows the country. Where do you think I'd stand? In a bread-line, that's where."

Naughton pushed his hat back, slumped lower in the seat. "If Quale's guilty, then there's got to be a pay-off," he said slowly. "There's no other way we can break the case without giving Maurice Quale a chance to do just that. If you get the check now, we can take it out there and tail him until we find out where the tie-up is."

Logan hesitated a full three minutes. Finally he tossed his cigarette butt out into the street. "O.K., Naughton, we'll play it your way."

Naughton turned on the ignition, said, "Swell!"

HE DROVE across town in silence, finally wheeled the roadster to the curb in front of the State Mutual Building.

"You can't very well get that check through this afternoon, can you?" he asked the insurance op. "Anyhow, Quale wouldn't be able to cash it if you did. Not today."

"Will it make a difference?"

"A hell of a difference!" Naughton admitted. "If my hunch is right, this case is going to explode in our faces."

Logan winced. "Well, we can make it. I think I can get the check through in about an hour; the company's waiting for my recommendation before paying off."

"But the banks will be closed. I had a hunch that if Quale could get some ready cash perhaps something would break."

"That's what I'm getting at," Logan interposed. "Quale banks at the Day and Night Bank—you know, it's open all hours. I discovered that when I was trying to find out about his financial standing. He's practically broke right now."

"Swell. Go up to your office and sit tight until you hear from me. Meanwhile, you get that check ready, get it certified, if you can, to speed things up. Right?"

Logan sighed, climbed out to the sidewalk. "I don't know whether I'm the sap or you are, but I'll see to it." He swung on his heel and stalked through the open bronze doors into the building.

NAUGHTON STARTED the roadster, swung left at the first intersection and drove south for ten blocks before he turned right again. He parked, walked half a block and into the Acme Sporting Palace.

The Acme was a two-storied joint. The main floor was filled with slot machines and other sucker devices; the upstairs was a gym where a lot of second-rate pushers worked out. There was a bowling-alley in the basement. In the center of the ground floor was a wicker-wire cage where a peaked-faced man with a bald head and a green eye-shade changed currency into nickels, dimes and quarters. There were two telephone booths at the end of the hall.

Naughton cashed a five into small change and satisfied himself there was a telephone in the wicker cage. Then he threw away a dollar in one of the machines, walked to the end of the massive room and into the right-hand booth, from the inside of which he could observe the man in the cage. Then he called the number of the Acme Sporting Palace.

Through the glass door of the booth, he saw the guy with the green eye-shade reach for the instrument, saw his lips move and at the same time the receiver at his ear debouched a crisp, "Hello?"

"I want to speak to Sam," Naughton announced.

"Who's this?" the cashier wanted to know.

"A friend of Nifty."

"Hold the wire!"

Watching, Naughton saw the man in the cage whistle. A pimply faced kid strolled up from the bowling-alley, went over to the cage. The cashier said something, the boy nodded and disappeared up the staircase toward the gym.

He came back in a couple of minutes heeled by a fat, swart man that looked like a Greek. The latter waddled up to the cage, reached his hand through the wicket window and pulled out the phone. His mouth moved up and down and a voice over the wire told Naughton: "This is Sam speakin'!"

The arson dick turned his back to the door, spoke quietly.

"Sam, this is Naughton. I want to get in touch with Nifty. Is he around?"

The Greek cleared his throat into the mouthpiece, then, "He ain't here. If he comes in, can I have him call you?"

"This is important," Naughton growled. "Can you reach him?"

"Maybe he'll come in," Sam grunted indifferently. "You want to leave a number, or maybe a message?"

"Tell him Naughton wants to see him right away. I'll meet him in the lobby of the Harrison. Have you got that? Don't have him call me, just be there." He looked out the door.

Sam the Greek was nodding his head. "Okie doke, Mr. Naughton. I'll tell him he should meet you right away in the lobby of the Harrison Hotel… if I should perhaps see him."

Naughton hung up, but stayed in the booth. He saw Sam talking to the pimply faced youth and when the boy nodded and turned toward the street door, the arson dick eased out of the booth and left the building by a side entrance. When he reached the main drag, the boy was heading west. Naughton crossed the street and followed.

The boy walked three blocks turned the corner onto Grant, and Naughton almost missed him as he vanished into the maw of a cheap apartment house. The detective cut diagonally across the street, pulled his hat low over his features and walked into the building.

The place had a mere widening in the hall for a lobby. A staircase leading up from it stretched then into one long corridor, with doors leading off both sides. The messenger was not in evidence.

NAUGHTON WALKED down to the far end of the corridor and found another staircase. He climbed to the second floor, paused, and saw the kid tramping down the front stairs from the third floor. He waited until the boy passed out of sight, then he hot-footed it up another flight. As he topped the landing, he saw Jobelman slip out of a door and head for the front stairs.

Naughton grinned, hung back out of sight and waited. In a minute he went to the door through which Jobelman had come. Making sure the corridor was deserted, he listened. The place seemed completely silent. He took a large ring of keys from his pocket, began testing them in the lock. The fifth one opened the door and Naughton eased inside, closing the panel softly after him.

The place looked innocent enough, and there was no evidence of any feminine hand. Through the half-open door of a bedroom, the arson dick saw an unmade bed and a chair with various masculine garments hanging over it. There was a chest of drawers, the top of which was littered with brilliant-hued ties.

There was another door, partly ajar, that opened into a small kitchen. A third door was closed. That would be the bathroom.

The living-room in which he found himself was cheaply furnished. There was a small circular table in the middle of a worn rug. There were several chairs, none of them inviting, all of them worn. Against one wall was a large, battered trunk. Naughton went over to it, found it locked.

He went down on one knee, took out his keys and started to look through the collection. Abruptly he froze.

A furtive scratching sound emanated from beyond the closed door. The detective dropped the keys in his pocket, unholstered his gun and stood up. His soft-soled shoes were soundless as he crossed the room.

The scratching stopped as he came up to the door. With his ear against the panel, Naughton thought he detected the hiss of heavy breathing. He tightened his grip on the gun, held it close to his body—and pushed open the door!

A long, dark form hurtled through the narrow opening, struck his chest and they went down together. Naughton clubbed his gun, struck once, then paused. The greyhound tumbled sideways, bounded to his feet and reared for another spring. Naughton, on one knee, raised his gun, then lowered it. The dog was muzzled, therefore harmless.

When the animal sprang at him again, Naughton pushed the helpless head aside and gripped the heavy harness. Thus held, the dog could do nothing but squirm and growl.

Naughton hung on until he made sure the apartment was otherwise empty, then he examined the unwilling hound. It was a beautiful beast, long, slender, and mostly black. He was about to shove it back into the tiny bathroom when he noticed a small gold nameplate on the harness. He looked closer, read the dog's name—*Battle-Cry.*

Todd Naughton whistled softly. He gave the dog a pat on the head, thrust it back into the bathroom and closed the door. He didn't bother with the trunk now. Instead, he made sure the room was as he found it, then walked into the corridor and locked the door behind him.

There was a strange, faraway light in his eyes as he hurried from the building and headed toward his parked roadster.

CHAPTER FIVE
EYEWITNESS

NIFTY JOBELMAN was restlessly waiting near the entrance in the Harrison lobby. When Naughton swung through the doors, he walked swiftly to meet the arson dick, whispered, "Let's get out of here, copper!" and went outside.

Naughton followed, indicating his roadster with a nod of his head. Jobelman went to it, climbed in.

When Naughton joined him, the informer said: "Well, did you get me some dough?"

The dick grinned. "Practically. The insurance company will pay. But we want some more information, Nifty. We can't make a pinch on what we know, not yet, anyhow."

Jobelman was plainly nervous. "Listen, copper, I ain't no mine. I gave you all I know."

Naughton stroked his chin, stared out the windshield. "There's just two things I'd like to know: who was the dead guy and—what happened to Nina Quale's greyhound."

Jobelman stiffened perceptibly, then shrugged. "Are they going to pinch Quale, or pay off?"

"I think they're going to pay the policy."

Jobelman hesitated. "Listen, Naughton, this town'll be pretty hot for me if and when they knock over Quale. He's got friends, see. If I got any dough coming from you, let's have it so I can take a powder if the goin' gets rough."

Naughton nodded. "You be where I can reach you tonight. I'll have something for you. I'm going to see the insurance outfit right away."

The informer ducked out of the car with alacrity. "Call Sam when you get it," he whined. "I'll keep in touch with him." He flashed a nervous smile and ducked into the passing current of pedestrians.

Naughton grimaced, and drove over to the State Mutual office. Logan was waiting, looking worried.

"They put it right up to me," he told Naughton with a grim smile. "This'd better work out right. They know the blaze was incendiary and they wanted to hold off payment until we completed our investigation. It took a lot of talking."

"But you got it."

"Fifty G's—certified."

"We'd better take your buggy," Naughton suggested. "That red paint on mine makes too much noise."

They went down to the street, crossed it and wheeled Logan's sedan out of a basement garage. The insurance op drove swiftly, silent, his forehead wrinkled moodily.

Naughton didn't feel much like talking; he was satisfied. He had all the pieces to the jig-saw puzzle—all save one. Perhaps that one'd complete the picture, make sense. Perhaps it wouldn't. The one thing he couldn't figure was the dead man. That didn't jibe, somehow. The rest of it didn't fit together perfectly either, because of it, but the arson dick felt satisfied they were onto something now.

The sedan stopped before the Haycox Hotel. "I telephoned," Logan said. "Quale's expecting us."

They went in and up. Maurice Quale opened the door of the suite. He greeted them both, invited them inside. But his manner was cool, reserved, even distant.

Logan came right to the point. He took the check from his pocket, handed it to the older man. "Certified for fifty thousand, Mr. Quale." He spread a receipt form on the table, offered a fountain pen. "I understand, sir, your loss exceeds the amount of the policy. I'm sorry to hear that"

Quale accepted both the check and the pen. As he leaned over to scrawl his signature on the receipt, he remarked: "Did you identify the body found near my office?"

Logan shot a quick glance at Naughton. The arson dick answered: "Not yet. But we will eventually. By the way, Mr. Quale, where is *Battle-Cry?*"

Quale returned the pen to Logan. He met Naughton's eyes. "Why do you ask that?"

Naughton's smile was enigmatic. "Curious."

Quale made no comment. He turned to Logan and formally thanked him for the check. Naughton had to admire the cool nerve of the man. If Maurice Quale was tied into an arson plot, he failed to show any external evidence of it.

THEY WENT back outside, climbed into the sedan. Logan turned on the ignition, said: "Now what?"

"Drive naturally to the first corner, turn right—then drive like hell around the block and park where we can watch this place."

Logan lifted an inquiring eyebrow but followed instructions, drove off. "Cool as hell!" he said admiringly. "Say, what's your interest in that mutt greyhound?"

"I was wondering if Quale knows where it is."

Logan brought the sedan to a stop in front of a delicatessen store. He slumped in his seat, rested the back of his head against the top of the seat cushion. "You know, Naughton," he observed moodily, "sometimes I can't figure you out. Do you work by a sense of smell, or are you just plain psychic. There's no logic to you."

Naughton grinned. "Don't get too damn comfortable." he suggested drily. "There's a cab pulling up at the Quale dug-out."

Logan jerked erect. They watched, saw the driver get out and disappear. He returned, waited, and then a girl ran out of the building, cast a quick glance up and down the street and dove into the tonneau.

Naughton whistled softly. "That's Nina Quale. Get this buggy rolling."

Logan swore softly, kicked the motor awake and as the cab eased into motion, he followed.

"Take it easy," Naughton warned the other. "That gal's wide awake."

Logan nodded and hung well back. The cab proceeded at a normal speed and they had no trouble tailing it to the downtown section where it pulled up in front of the Day and Night Bank. The girl left the cab and disappeared through the revolving door of the bank. The cab stayed at the curb.

Logan slowed. "Now what?"

Naughton gestured to a parking-place in front of a fire-plug. When the insurance op tooled the sedan into the spot and stopped, Naughton said; "Nina Quale knows me by sight so I can't follow her into that bank. You can. Hike in there, nail the cashier or the first big-shot handy and find out what she does with that check."

Logan slid into the street. "What do you expect her to do?"

Naughton frowned. "She's going to cash it or some of it. But make it snappy. The cab's waiting for her and it's a cinch she's not going home. When she leaves, I'll start after her and pick you up as we roll past the bank. We don't want to lose her."

Logan hurried down the sidewalk, passed into the bank.

NAUGHTON LIT a cigarette, his eyes on the heavy doors. Suppose he was guessing wrong. Suppose—

The Quale girl literally dove out of the bank and into the cab. It moved away at once.

Naughton rolled the sedan away from the curb as the cab ducked into the stream of traffic. He had a few anxious seconds wondering if he had better wait for Logan, or beat it after the cab. As he slowed in passing the bank, the insurance op dashed out into the street, hopped onto the running-board and swung himself into the front seat as Naughton gassed the car ahead.

"You rang a bull's-eye!" Logan panted. "She's got ten thousand in cash with her now!"

Naughton smiled grimly. The cab was weaving in and out of traffic at a good clip. Ten blocks from the bank, it made a sharp left turn. Naughton followed. Four blocks further it swung right, and as the arson dick went into the same turn, he glimpsed the cab doubling left. Naughton speeded up, made the turn and saw the cab batting in a straight line.

Logan swore again. "Looks like she made us!"

Naughton depressed the accelerator, and the sedan began to close the gap that separated it from the cab.

Logan said: "Hell, man! If she hasn't spotted us now she sure will!"

Naughton growled, began to overtake the taxi. The driver seemed indifferent. In two more blocks they drew alongside.

Logan nearly jumped out of the sedan. "She's gone! There's nobody in the cab!" he gasped out.

Naughton pulled over to the curb. "That's what I was afraid of. She tricked us. She ducked out on one of those turns."

Logan groaned; his shoulders drooped. "Gone! With ten grand of our dough! Well, I hope you're convinced that Quale's the guy we want. Let's go back and get him before we lose the other forty G's."

Naughton threw in the clutch and as the sedan jerked ahead, he chuckled. "Why in hell didn't I think of it before!" He shot around the first corner and drove at top speed across the city.

Logan groaned again. "What's the gag?"

Naughton didn't answer. He rocketed around a beer truck, straightened, turned another corner and went south. Five minutes later he skidded around a turn onto Grant, swung in to the curb and stopped. There was a cab at the curb in front of Jobelman's apartment house, the engine running. Naughton punched open the car door and dove out. "Come on," he told Logan.

The insurance operative followed.

Naughton walked swiftly into the building, heeled by Logan, tramped down the corridor and started up the rear stairs. As their heads came level with the third floor, Naughton held up his hand for a pause.

The insurance op sucked the air through clenched teeth, started to ask a question, when they heard the faint, sharp cry of a woman. Logan started up the stairs, but Naughton held him back.

"Wait!" he ordered.

The door of Nifty Jobelman's suite banged open and Nina Quale slipped furtively into the hall. She threw a terrified glance about her, but the two detectives were hidden in a pool of shadow. As she fled toward the front stairs, Naughton saw that she was carrying a dog's blanket and harness.

A puzzled frown darkened his face. The girl had barely disappeared when he ran down the hallway, pushed open the door of the apartment. He jerked to an abrupt halt. Logan, peering over his shoulder, said: "Oh, my God!"

Jobelman lay on his back, blood smeared over his face. The greyhound, skull smashed, was draped across one arm. A wrecked chair and an overturned table gave evidence of a battle royal.

"She killed him!" Logan asserted.

Naughton dropped on one knee beside the slim informer, pushed a sensitive hand inside his shirt. "He's not dead yet!" he told Logan. "Grab that dame!"

The other tore out of the suite.

Naughton started to pull the dog off the wounded man, stopped suddenly. He cast a quick, suspicious glance about the apartment, rose and jerked open the hall door. He shouted, "I'm coming, Logan!" then slammed the door. After that, he jerked out his revolver, tip-toed back of the davenport.

A door opened; a man eased into the room. He held a bloody gun clubbed in his right hand. He went over to the man on the floor, started a hurried search of his clothing, cursing as he worked, but apparently found nothing that interested him. He rose, then bent swiftly and jerked off Jobelman's right shoe. Under an inner-sole, he found what he wanted. A small piece of cardboard!

He thrust this into a side pocket, picked up his gun and raised it above Jobelman's skull.

Naughton stepped out, said: "Hold it, Bennet!"

Simon Bennet whirled, flung the gun at Naughton's head and followed it with a dive. Naughton sidestepped, swung his left fist. It collided with Bennet's jaw. The book-keeper slid gracefully to the floor, cold.

Logan pushed open the door. He had Nina Quale by the wrist.

The insurance op saw Bennet. "Say, where'd he come from?"

Naughton stooped, removed the tiny slip of cardboard from the bookkeeper's pocket. It was a baggage claim-check from a branch depot of the railroad about ten blocks away. He pocketed it, gave Logan a grim smile—and his handcuffs.

"Neither of these birds are dead," he said. "Take 'em down to the police emergency hospital at headquarters. I'll meet you there."

Logan was stuttering out another question as Naughton went through the door.

TWENTY-FIVE MINUTES later, Todd Naughton pushed into headquarters wearing a knowing grin and lugging a heavy suitcase. The desk-sergeant smiled. "Your party's holdin' out in Sergeant Kane's office," he told Naughton. "He's wild to know where you are. Ain't leavin' us?" He glanced at the suitcase.

Naughton chuckled, wagged his head and tramped down the dingy corridor to the homicide bureau. They were all there, obviously waiting for him. Kane glowered at him.

"Well, well! You been on a vacation someplace?" he growled.

The arson dick let his eyes wander over the assemblage. Maurice Quale stood behind a chair in which his daughter, Nina, was seated.

Kovack loafed against the desk nearby as though he suspected the Quales might bolt. Logan, too, stood grimly near the door. He was worried about the company's fifty G's.

In two swivel chairs placed facing each other in the middle of the room, Simon Bennet and Nifty Jobelman slumped.

There was nothing "nifty" about the slim Jobelman. His head was turbaned with bandages and his garish clothing was stained with dried blood. His face, twitching nervously, was an incongruous blending of rage and fear. He squinted angrily at Naughton, then his eyes dropped to the suitcase in the detective's hand. His jaw sagged.

Naughton heaved the suitcase onto the desk beside Kane. Simon Bennet, watching him, shot a quick, venomous glance at the little informer and his shoulders went limp. He looked old and very tired.

Naughton turned to the bookie. "The key, Nifty?" He held out his hand.

Jobelman shrugged, fished a key-ring out of his pocket and dropped it in the outstretched hand. "It's the little flat one," he admitted resignedly.

Naughton opened the suitcase while the others crowded around. It contained three large ledgers.

Maurice Quale grunted sharply. "Why those are the account books of the track!"

Naughton nodded, turned to Jobelman. "Talk, Nifty?"

Kane swung around. "So, you little rat, you done it, eh?"

Nifty licked dry lips, edged closer to Naughton. "Like hell I did!" he whined. "It was Si Bennet! He'd been robbing the till doing his betting with me. I got an idea he was juggling the account books an' when I found out that Guy Poole was planning to grab the track, I figured Bennet would have to do something or be discovered when the new regime went in. I saw him set the fire to burn up the books, and when he beat it, I ducked in and saved them."

"So you could blackmail Bennet?"

Jobelman's mouth twitched. "Well," he whined, "a guy's got to eat."

Nina Quale sobbed aloud. "Oh, Simon! We trusted you so!"

Naughton turned to the girl, "Bennet was caught in his own net. He couldn't take the books away without immediately drawing suspicion on himself. He had to burn the track to burn the books and so cover his embezzlements. Do you mind explaining why you took *Battle-Cry* away from the track just before the fire, and how he came to be in Jobelman's possession?"

THE GIRL shrugged. "He was my pet," she whispered. "I knew that Poole meant to grab the track and I didn't want him to get *Battle-Cry*. I took him away.

"After the fire, suspicion was turned against father. Jobelman came to me and told me that the police had questioned him and that they planned to arrest father. He insinuated that he knew who did set the fire, however, and their motive. He offered me this information for ten thousand dollars.

"I was desperate, but I did not have that sum. He suggested I leave the dog with him until I could turn up the money. As soon as father received the check, I went down to claim the dog and get the information that would prove who had set the fire. I came into the apartment and found Jobelman and my—" She dropped her face into her hands.

"Just one more question, Miss Quale," Naughton asked. "You took the harness so you would not be connected with Jobelman?"

"I thought he was dead!"

Simon Bennet lifted his head. "There is no use prolonging this," he muttered huskily. "I was desperate, Maurice." He addressed his statement to the track-owner. "I did not realize how I was hurting you until I was in so deep I couldn't get out. Jobelman milked me, but I'm not blaming him. I couldn't stand the thought of exposure so I fired the track. I knew you would get the insurance and I thought it was better than losing the track to Poole. When the police grabbed Watkins, I became terrified. I had a shyster get him out on bail, then I—"

"You killed him!" Kane put in bluntly.

Bennet nodded. "I meant to kill Jobelman, too. He's a dirty, double-crossing little rat. But I didn't mean to kill your dog, Miss Nina! Honest! I'm so shortsighted, however, that when he leapt at me, I couldn't see that he was muzzled." He hung his head.

Kane climbed down from the desk, took a slow turn around the room. "You know," he broke the silence, "I got called into this case because there was a dead guy found in a closet. I hate to be inquisitive," he added sarcastically, "but after all, I'm workin' homicides. Ain't I, Kovack?"

The Pole nodded somberly. "Sure. The sarge an' me're workin' homicides, so somebody better tell us about the dead guy."

Nifty worked nervous lips. "I don't know nothin' about that, s'help me—"

Bennet shrugged his shoulders. "I shot him, dragged him into the closet," he admitted wearily. "I don't know who he was, but when I came running out of the office after setting off the fuse, he was coming straight toward me with a heavy stick in his hand. He was looking straight at me.

He would have been an eyewitness, so it was him or me. I—killed him!"

Kane bit his lip. "But who was he? What did he look like? We gotta identify him!"

Bennet hung his head, spoke very low.

"I just have a half-vague impression. He was about my age, a checkered suit, a slouch hat pulled down all around—"

Jobelman jerked erect, half screamed: "A heavy stick you said...?"

Bennet nodded. The little informer gripped his chair, turned horrified eyes on the arson dick.

"No wonder we had such God-awful luck!" he sobbed out. "He didn't kill no eyewitness—that was Old Joe, the blind beggar!"

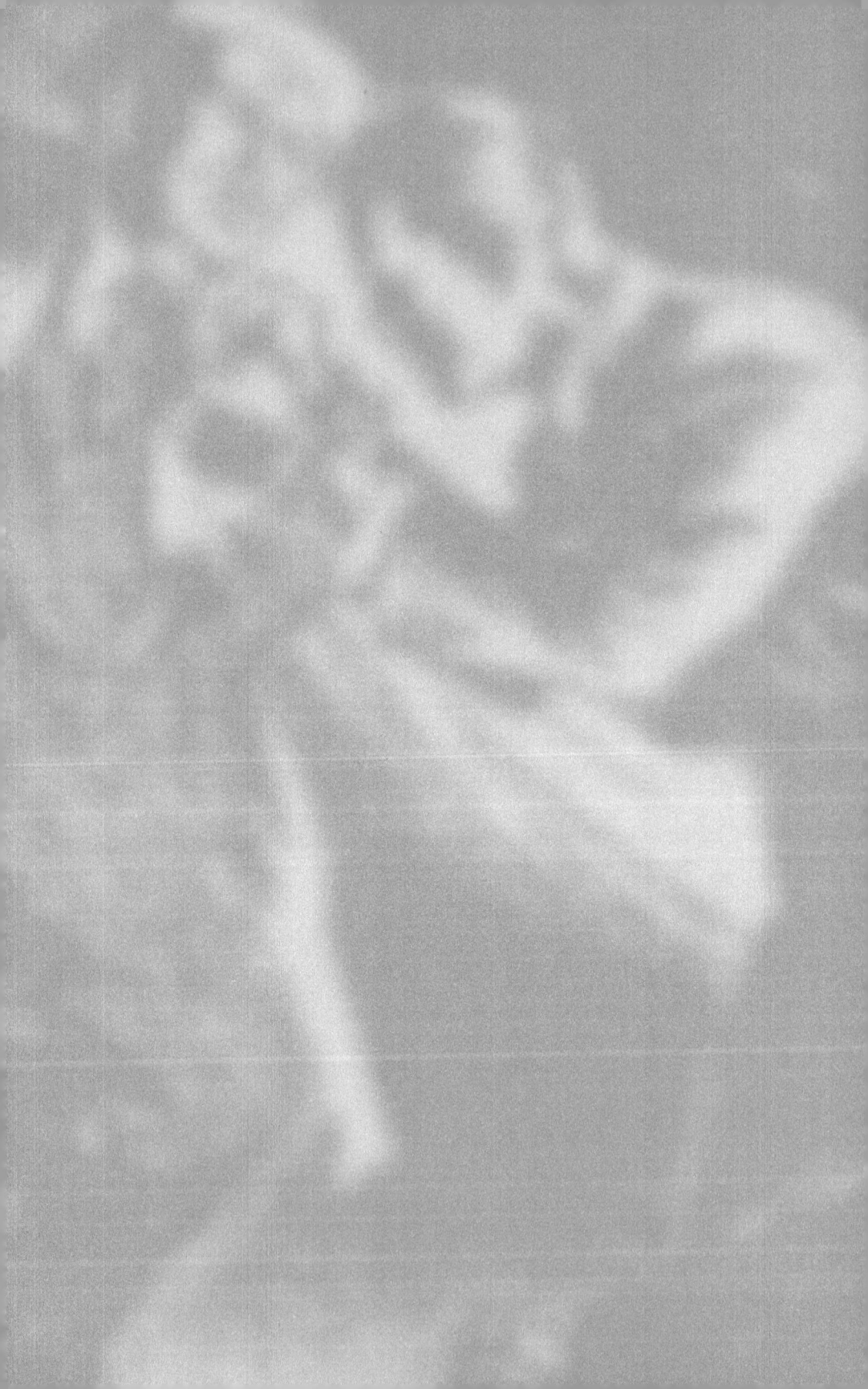

ASHES OF THE LIVING

THREE CHARRED AND BLACKENED BODIES WERE THE ONLY CLUE TO THE IDENTITY OF THE ARSON-KILLER WHO HAD KINDLED THAT ANCIENT FIRE-TRAP. AND TODD NAUGHTON, INVESTIGATING THE MURDER-BLAZE, FOUND HIS JOB DOUBLY DIFFICULT WHEN ONE OF THOSE HUMAN CORPSE-TORCHES SUDDENLY SPRANG ALIVE.

CHAPTER ONE
PYRE FOR THE LIVING

NAUGHTON HELD the hurtling roadster astraddle the trolley-tracks, so that he might have a choice of either side of the street in case of an impending crash.

The long red eye of the official spotlight danced ahead of his boring headlights, like the inquisitive finger of some monster, prehistoric beetle. Only once did the arson dick risk the use of his siren and then merely to growl it sufficiently for the traffic-bull stationed at Market and Wall to clear the intersection. While the big cop semaphored traffic out of the way, Naughton caromed into a squealing left-hand turn onto Market, flashed three blocks and rolled right into a small side street. As he steadied the roadster, he reached up, switched off the tell-tale spotlight. He almost glided the two remaining blocks, tooling to the curb in front of a small neighborhood pharmacy.

Before the red roadster slid to a full stop, a man sprang out of a shadowed areaway and jumped on the running-board. His lean young body was wrapped in a trench-coat which flapped around his legs from the wind. A crush felt hid the upper part of his face, but not the taut lips, nor the square-sculptured jaw.

"You made it, Naughton!" he rasped excitedly. "We'll catch 'em red-handed this time! Drag your freight out of this heap."

The arson dick yanked on the emergency, shunted his rangy, loose-jointed frame to the sidewalk and spun a glowing cigarette butt into the gutter. He grinned at the younger man. There was a boyish eagerness about the ambitious insurance investigator that Naughton admired.

"All right, Ralph," he growled good-naturedly. "Where's the spot, and who've you got cornered?"

Ralph Hunt moved impatiently.

"There isn't time for details," he snapped. "It's that joint over there." He indicated a two-storied frame house halfway down the block on the opposite side of the street. "I was afraid you wouldn't get here in time and I'd have to make the knock-over alone."

Naughton scowled.

"Lay off the solo stuff. Professional fire-bugs are tough customers. We should have more men, as it is."

"Men, hell! The torch went into the house nearly ten minutes ago. He'll be coming out any minute. This pinch means a lot to me, Naughton; I've got to make it stick. That's why I called you." He started moving rapidly along the sidewalk, hugging the shadows.

Naughton started to follow, then his sharp eyes picked up the outline of a figure crouched in a darkened car parked across the street. He stretched long legs in a quick stride, caught Hunt's arm.

"There's someone in that coupé!"

The insurance op nodded. "My girl," he admitted with a quick smile. "We were on our way to the theater when I picked up this tail. She insisted on coming along."

They hurried to a position opposite the two-storied house, paused in a pool of darkness while the arson dick studied the place with appraising eyes.

He catapulted him into the
white hell of the oven.

THE STRUCTURE was ripe for a touch-off; a typical
fire trap of age-dried wood, which, if ignited, would
become a massive pyre for the unfortunate smoke-eaters
who might have to venture inside. The detective's glance
flashed up and down the street, instinctively gauging the
distances to the hydrants, judging the velocity of the wind,
the chance of a spread.

Hunt nudged him.

"Let's go," he pleaded, "before he gets away. You take the
front. I want to cover the back. He'll probably come out
that way, and I need this pinch, fella."

Naughton frowned.

"We've got to give him a chance to touch-off a blaze, kid. You can't make an arson case until the fire has actually started."

"I know, I know," argued the other man. "But I tell you he's at work. See you later," and before Naughton could restrain him, he ducked across the street to disappear up the cement driveway between the houses.

The arson dick waited until he was sure the insurance op had reached his objective. He transferred his revolver from a shoulder holster to the pocket of his topcoat, squinted at the house on the other side of the street. At first it appeared totally dark, but finally his eyes picked up the sliver of yellow light limning one of the windows on the second floor. He crossed the street diagonally, made the shelter of a telephone pole.

A nebulous premonition of disaster stirred him. Naughton was not given to nerves and he tried to shake the sensation. He decided it was young Hunt's inexperience which worried him. He shouldn't let the kid hit the back, for that's where the trouble would come; but he knew, too, what a successful pinch would mean to Ralph. Promotion, more money, which in turn meant marriage. Naughton grinned in spite of himself, grinned a little wistfully. Ralph, he knew, was very much in love.

Abruptly, the smile faded into a thin-lip line. The bristles on his nape came erect. He had his gun out and was pumping his long legs toward the front door when the structure exploded in his face. The blast plucked him clear of the ground, flung him back. His shoulders landed first, jarring the wind out of him. He skidded along the sidewalk and came to rest with his head propped against the curb of the cement drive.

THE ROAR numbed his hearing, dazed him. But his mind pinwheeled so feverishly it seemed to gear the ghastly drama down to slow motion. Helpless, he saw the lower walls sucked inward while those of the upper story bulged out. Simultaneously, the roof lifted as if jacked up by the solid shaft of flame which followed. Against this backdrop of fire the stiffened body of a man catapulted from the inferno in an arc that terminated, head down, on the unyielding pavement of the driveway. The skull spattered like an egg-shell.

Naughton stumbled erect.

"Ralph! Ralph!" he screamed hoarsely, and made a run for the limp figure.

But the flames refused to surrender their victim. With a sickening *whoosh* they sucked downward, seared the hair from Naughton's face, and drove him back.

The arson dick sobbed, threw a protecting arm over his features and retreated to the street. He looked around. The detonation had shattered every window in sight, and sparsely clad people came streaming out of shaken houses near by.

Naughton suppressed the nausea that gripped him. Remembering he was still a cop, he grabbed the first man who panted up, sent him to flash an alarm. As he turned back, he glimpsed the slight figure of a girl race toward the burning building.

"Hey, you fool!" he shouted, and when she did not stop took after her.

She made for the dark mound in the alley now flicked by the long whip-ends of flame. One darting tongue touched her, and the flowing dress ignited just as the arson dick reached her. He flung her to the ground, fell across her with his flopping coat and rolled her savagely. Then he scooped her into his arms and made a dash for the street.

He made it, but his coat was afire. He shoved the screaming girl into the arms of a fat policeman who had pounded up, wrestled out of his coat and threw it away.

"Let me go!" shrieked the girl. "He's lying there! For God's sake let me get him!"

The big copper looked at Naughton. The dick nibbled his singed lip.

"Who is he?"

"Ralph Hunt!" she screamed and clawed at the officer. "You deliberately sent him in there!" This accusation was thrown at Naughton.

Naughton winced, swiveled. He couldn't tell her the truth, that if the body was her fiancé, he was already dead.

"He's being burned alive!" the girl wailed. "You stand here and watch!" She struggled frantically.

NAUGHTON GESTURED for the cop to hold her tight, tried to work his way closer to the body. The starless night was hideous with the yellow-and-scarlet flames which splashed the scene. Already the clothing on the corpse was smouldering. It was hopeless.

Sirens wailed from two directions. Naughton, face black and raw, jostled his way through the now morbid crowd. He was guided by the beacon of the girl's cries.

"It's impossible," he managed. "I tried!"

A caterwauling ambulance charged through the crowd, skidded to a quick stop near by.

"You sent him there!" reiterated the hysterical girl. "He took all the risk while you hid behind a pole out front." She was staring at Naughton with distended eyes. "You murdered him!"

Naughton wiped away the charred flakes that had once been his eyelashes, gulped air into his seared lungs. He felt guilty enough, yet he couldn't tell her his reason for letting young Hunt take the back was to give the lad a chance to earn a promotion that would mean marriage to him and to her. He turned away, beckoned the white-clad interne who was swinging out of the ambulance.

"This girl has just witnessed her fiancé die," he snapped. "Take her to the emergency and give her something to quiet her nerves before she cracks completely." He jerked away to meet the skipper of Number 8 Company which had arrived simultaneously with the ambulance.

Captain Jensen was already waving his great arms while he bawled his commands.

"Hook up that pumper! Lay a line around the rear. Hey, Swede, ladder the north side of the building." He saw the arson dick. "Hello, Naughton, you got here in one hell of a hurry!"

"There were some people in that house!" Naughton rasped. "One body was blown clear, landed in the drive over there. I tried to reach it."

Jensen strode as close as he dared, shielding his pitted old face with an elbow.

"I can't send a man over there!" he bellowed, trying to make himself audible above the din. "Not until the asbestos squad gets here. He's roasted, anyhow. Know who it was?"

Naughton flinched, nodded.

"I'm afraid it is young Hunt, of the Interstate Mutual."

Jensen swore. "That blond kid… Ralph Hunt? Hell, what was he doing in there?"

"It was a touch-off. Hunt had a tip of some kind—there wasn't time to explain. He called me tonight, told me a torch was at work and to high-ball over here and help him. When I arrived, he was too impatient to give details. He wanted to make the pinch himself, so he insisted on hitting the rear. I gave him time to get set, started for the front. She went up." He made a descriptive gesture with his hands.

"God!" half prayed the old smoke-eater. "An' the torch?"

Naughton shrugged. "I never saw him."

Somebody shouted for the skipper. Jensen bawled his position, turned.

"We can't do anything till that blaze is licked," he growled, and moved away.

Naughton mingled with the crowd, studied faces, but somehow he could not tear himself very far away from the blackened corpse in the drive. One of the paramount rules for an arson dick is, when on the scene of a blaze, to watch the crowd, not the fire. That's the way to spot a torch—a criminal that ignites fires. But tonight Todd Naughton did not feel like an arson detective. He felt like a murderer.

He wondered if the orthodox hell could be as agonizing as this. The flames blistered his face and his feet were cold from the hose-spray. The crackle of the flame, the "Oh's" and "Ah's" of the crowd, the hoarse cries of the firemen— and over it all the steady thunder of the giant pumper.

The building did not last long. Two more companies arrived, and finally the flames died, became smoke. The blaze lost its vivacity, its life, and became drab, dirty, miserable. The crowd thinned as the glamor disappeared. Then in the half-light, Naughton watched the asbestos squad march up. Clad in suits of gray asbestos, faces hidden under goggled masks, the five figures minced into the gutted structure. As they merged with the thick smoke, licked at by dying flames, Naughton had a dizzy sensation of unreality.

THEY DISAPPEARED through the door-way, and occasionally he caught glimpses of them moving through the grimy fog, like hypothetical Martians. Then they reappeared at the entrance, staggered out with two ghastly objects. A weak cry went up from the crowd.

"Bodies! Corpses!"

Naughton hurried over as the ghost-men deposited their awful burdens beyond the lines. He looked, turned quickly away. The unforgettable stench of burned flesh nauseated him. The coroner's men claimed the charred remains.

The blaze was a complete success—from the torch's point of view. Practically nothing of the doomed building remained. That was the trouble with arson; the fire itself collaborated with the criminal to destroy the evidence. Naughton decided to go back to headquarters. It would be hours before he could enter the ruins to make his routine search, and he expected nothing from it.

He slopped through the puddles of water that filled each depression in the sidewalk, trudged toward his car in front of the small drug-store. Even the little red roadster was covered with a thin layer of ash-dust. His throat burned and he glanced through the lighted window of the store to see if they were serving coffee at the fountain. The place was obviously closing, and Naughton was about to turn away, when he came face to face with a man who came running out of the drugstore.

At sight of Naughton, the man jerked up short, gaped with terrified eyes. He was a squat figure, hatless and bald, barrel-shaped.

Naughton rasped, "Mose Vogel!" and started forward.

Vogel gave a yelp of fear, jumped back into the store, slammed the door in the detective's face. Naughton went down to one knee, stumbling erect in time to see the fat man streaking toward the rear of the store.

The detective yanked out his gun, tried the door and when he found it locked, smashed an opening in the glass for his arm. He reached inside, opened the door, barged in. Ignoring the squeals of the indignant druggist, he charged through the narrow store just as Vogel bolted through a rear door into an alley.

Mose Vogel made good time for a fat man, but Naughton's long legs pumped him closer with every stride. He could have shot the galloping figure, but he wanted him alive.

Vogel started to lean around a corner, realizing he was running a lost race and whirled at bay. He came around fighting, and he took the detective by surprise. A wild swing caught Naughton in the stomach, doubled him momentarily. He closed with Vogel, jostled him against the brick wall of a building, and, tossing his gun aside, began to push punches like a riveting-machine. Vogel shuddered under each impact, tried to worm away. His hysterical effort expended, he sobbed his surrender as he sagged down the wall to the ground.

Naughton gave him an extra wallop in the jaw to relax him, rolled him over and cuffed his wrists behind him. He retrieved his gun, holstered it, then pulled Vogel to his feet.

"Got you, Vogal!" he snarled, "Got you cold! It's murder this time, as well as arson, and we'll make it stick."

Vogel shook as though palsied.

"I didn't do it! Honest before my God! I swear it to you, Mr. H'officer!"

Naughton hit him an open-handed slap across the mouth which straightened him against the wall.

"You lying rat!" he growled. "You killed a pal of mine on this job. Didn't do it, eh? What in hell are you doing in this neighborhood? Why'd you break and run when you saw me? Why did you fight?"

"I was passin'," the man moaned. "I... I went in the store to use the phone. When I saw you, well, I thought maybe you'd think I—" He floundered impotently.

Naughton gave his captive a hard, appraising stare. Mose Vogel's flabby jowls quivered with apprehension. His globular, vein-streaked eyes literally rolled in terror.

"We'll take a trip to headquarters," the dick growled ominously. "Maybe we can jolt the truth out of you." He twisted a black hand in Vogel's collar and dragged him around the corner of the alley to the roadster.

At the machine, Vogel balked again.

"I tell you I ain't guilty!" he bleated, and tried to run.

Naughton straight-armed him in the stomach, heaved him into the single seat. Then, while the prisoner blubbered his plea, Naughton stretched under the wheel, growled the motor alive and sirened his way to headquarters.

CHAPTER TWO
THREE ON A SLAB

IT WAS twenty minutes of midnight when Naughton rough-housed the reluctant Vogel down the battered corridor to Central Station into his own office. He rammed the prisoner into a substantial straight-backed chair.

"Now," he grated. "Well talk."

Vogel wagged his head. "Listen, h'officer, I got a right to a mouthpiece. I—" He stopped as Kane and Kovack, of the homicide squad, barged in.

Sergeant Kane squinted at Vogel, shunted his small eyes to the arson dick.

"What's the gag? You look like you was Al Jolson doin' a black-face. Don't he, Kovy?"

Kovack was built along the line of a bamboo pole, a loose-jointed, silent Pole who was able to work with the irascible sergeant for the sole reason that his speech was limited to a tardy echo of Kane's own words.

"Yah, it looks like a gag. Him with his face all black like Al Jolson. Hey, Sarge, who is Al Jolson?"

Naughton rubbed three fingers across his blistered face—and they came away soot streaked. He turned, crossed to a wash-bowl in a corner and doused his face with water.

"The coroner just buzzed me," Kane rumbled. "Said they found three stiffs in a fire. Arson, he said, so that sort of puts us in it together. What's the dope? This mugg got anything to do with it?" He sauntered across the office, leaned his back against the desk and began whittling his fingernails with a penknife.

Naughton patted his face with a paper towel. He looked at Kane, nibbled his lip. The homicide squad always horned in where a death occurred in an arson job, and Naughton was expected to work with them. It was a difficult job.

THIS KANE was a bunchy man with barrel-shaped torso and stumpy legs. He assumed a beefy, flabby stance for purposes of deception. Actually, he was well-conditioned, fast, and hard. Fiftyish, his features were ploughed in furrows of bitterness. But if he was tough and irritable, he was a good dick and an honest one, Naughton respected him for that.

"This rat is Mose Vogel," Naughton explained. "He was coming out of a store about a hundred and fifty yards from the fire. When he spotted me, he made a break for it. He put up a fight, when I caught up with him."

Kane regarded the prisoner with expressionless eyes.

"He must know you, eh, Naughton?"

"He should," the arson dick said. "I pinched him about fourteen months ago for burning up his tailor shop. I got an indictment, but that rotten little shyster Hugo Srack beat the rap for him. I'd like—"

"Some day," a mocking voice behind them commented, "you'll get sued for those statements, young man."

Naughton pirouetted, scowled at the slender little man framed in the doorway.

Kane's warped old mouth lifted in a smirk.

"Some day you'll get shot for opening doors without an invitation," he observed dryly.

"Well, Srack, what in hell do you want?" barked Naughton.

Srack dropped his brief-case on a chair, tipped his thinning gray head toward the quaking bulk of Vogel. "Mose telephoned me to meet him here. What's the idea of the handcuffs?"

Naughton exchanged glances with Kane.

"Vogel touched off a two-storied frame building on Hester Street tonight," he told the attorney. "Three men died, as a result."

"It ain't true!" Vogel shrieked. "I was calling you, Mr. Srack, when this h'officer grabbed me."

"You was expectin' a pinch, eh?" Kane commented.

"And what were you doing in that neighborhood?" Naughton demanded.

Vogel gulped, looked from one hard face to the other with stricken eyes.

"The house," he sobbed, "she was mine!"

"Yours?"

Vogel began to weep. "S'help me, I didn't fire it. I just—"

Srack held up a restraining hand.

"Take it easy," he cautioned. "Gentlemen, as counsel for Mr. Vogel, I must advise him against answering any further questions until I have had an opportunity to examine the case."

Kane breathed on his nails, rubbed them along his pants' leg. "Sure you must. You two got to figure out some perjury together."

"I ain't lyin'," wailed Vogel. "I tell everythin'. I rent my house to a man named Ritter. Tonight I get a call, tell me to come see about my house, so I—"

"Unless you stop right now," Srack put in tartly, "I won't take your case."

"What a break that would be, eh, Kovy?" Kane observed.

The Polack grinned. "Ya," he agreed, "what a break, eh, Sarge?"

"But I ain't guilty," sobbed the prisoner. "Why should I keep still? I don't know who—"

"Insured?" Naughton asked.

Vogel gulped, glanced at Srack. The attorney shrugged.

"You may as well answer that one," he admitted. "They'll find it out, anyhow."

Vogel hung his head. "Yes, it was insured."

Kane lowered one eye in a perceptible wink. "This Ritter what rented your dump. Who is he?"

"You may answer that one," Srack agreed.

Vogel wagged his head. "I dunno him. I put an ad in paper, an' he come to rent it. He is a little short fella about so high." He twisted his manacled wrists around to indicate a height from the floor.

Norton flexed his fingers, impatiently.

"I'm going to heave you in a can, Srack or no Srack," he told Vogel. "But if you have any out on this case it will be by playing ball. Now, I'm going to take you over to the morgue and we'll see if you can identify this man Ritter among the bodies they brought in."

Vogel began to shake harder. Srack gave him a professional pat on the shoulder. "Buck up, old chap," he soothed. "Hugo Srack will stand by you."

"That must be a great comfort," sneered Kane. "Come on, I'll roll you over to the meat shop in my buggy."

"What do you think," Naughton asked Kane during the ride.

"It's one-two-three," the sergeant assured him. "This mugg Vogel will crack before we get done with him."

THEY HAD trouble getting Mose Vogel to look at the corpses long enough to identify anything. Twice they led him up to the charred crisp lumps set on the white-porcelain drainage tables, and twice he went sick. "Got rid of at least three previous meals," as the sergeant phrased it.

Finally, however, he made a tentative identification of one corpse from the general outline. One of the two bodies carried out of the gutted house was short, about five feet. This stature fitted with Vogel's fragmentary description of the tenant, Ritter.

"There ain't much doubt," Kane observed. "Five feet is an unusual height in a grown man. Ritter rented the house, we find a five-foot corpse in the joint. It looks conclusive, eh, Kovy?"

"There ain't much doubt it's conclusive," Kovack admitted.

"Now, about the other two?" Kane wanted to know.

Naughton bit his lip, turned to the grim embers of what had been men but a few hours before. The one with the crushed skull, found in she alley, was only partly charred. All the clothing was burned off but the side of the body which had rested on the ground was not charred. However, Naughton could find nothing recognizable about it.

"I was called to the spot by young Ralph Hunt, an investigator for the Interstate Mutual," he said slowly, his eyes riveted on the body. "He thought the torch was in the house so he went around the rear, intending to break in and nab him at work. He was gone just a couple of minutes before the explosion, and I'm afraid—" He paused.

"If that body is Hunt," Srack put in, "and he went in after the torch, how can you tie my client into it?"

"Vogel may have sapped him and made his get-away," reasoned Kane.

The lawyer snorted. "Nonsense! That is pure supposition. By the same token, Ritter might have set the fire, assuming for the moment that it was arson at all—or this unidentified corpse may have been your mythical torch."

The morgue attendant spoke up.

"That don't make sense, because these two guys found inside the joint were evidently asleep in their beds. That's the way the rescue squad found 'em, anyhow."

"There's nothing to it," Kane growled decisively, "These two guys were in bed, an' Vogel set the blaze. Hunt surprises him when he's makin' his get-away, so Vogel smacks him and heats it. He knows he's been uncovered, so he calls you, Srack. Now, you want to lie him out of it."

"You can't bully me," the attorney sneered. "I'll laugh the crew of you out of a courtroom. Why, hell, you can't even prove it's arson. Any jury in the world would be reasonable enough to suppose that Ritter and this unknown man were asleep in their beds, and that the explosion was an accident."

"What about Hunt's tip?" Naughton reminded him,

Srack made a deprecatory gesture. "Since you cannot produce this man Hunt to testify, this yarn of yours is inadmissible as evidence. How do I know there ever was such a man as Hunt, or that he ever went near the house on Hester Street?"

Naughton balled his fists, took a half step toward the attorney.

"You rotten—"

Kane stopped him. "Smack him," the sergeant agreed, "but pick a time when there ain't so many witnesses around."

The attendant hissed a warning and hurriedly threw covers over the corpse-laden tables as the deputy coroner led a sobbing woman through a doorway at the far end of the white-tiled room. The detectives removed their hats, backed away from the tables, and watched the couple cross the room.

The coroner's deputy was an apologetic little man who had once studied to be an undertaker, but, lacking initiative required for private endeavor, had degenerated into politics. He had the soapy, ingratiating manner that is presumed to comfort the bereaved and he clung to the arm of the buxom woman, steering her like the clumsy rudder of a barge.

"Gentlemen," he whispered to the silent assemblage, "this is Mrs. Longstreth. Her dear husband was in the house on Hester Street when it burned. She wishes to try and make sure—"

NAUGHTON LOOKED at the woman. Expensive clothes hung on an hourglass figure and were crowned by a coiffure of synthetic blue-white. Her mouth was covered by a handkerchief, and she swept the men with large blue eyes, misted with tears. To the arson dick, she looked about forty, but she had obviously crowded a lot of living into the years.

"Where is he?" she sobbed huskily. "Oh, don't keep me in this awful suspense! Harold, oh, Harold!"

The deputy made a futile motion with his hands as if he didn't know what to do with them.

"My dear Mrs. Longstreth," he murmured. "The bodies are, well, terribly burned. Is there anything you could tell us-some mark, or perhaps the teeth?"

She covered her face with ring-decked fingers and sobbed audibly for a moment. Then she wound up with a long moan.

"Harold—my husband—had an old knife scar on his left wrist," she managed. "He also had a little five-pointed birthmark on his left hip. His teeth—he had dental work on his teeth. There was a silver filling on the anterior surface of the upper left first molar and a gold bridge on the lower right side, anchored to the first bicuspid and the first molar. That... that is all I can remember." She broke down again.

The morgue attendant gasped, "My God," and looked at Naughton. "That's the man they found in the alley!"

The woman gave a terrified bleat, and the deputy blinked his calf's-eyes.

"Are you sure, Dave?"

The attendant nodded vigorously, pulled back one of the table-covers. He pointed to a small red birthmark on the blued hip of the corpse.

"I just finished examining the teeth," he announced, "and it checks. Now if this is the birthmark…?"

Mrs. Longstreth braced herself, pulled down her handkerchief and bent close to the corpse. She stared for nearly a full minute, then screamed: "That's it! Oh, my God! My Harold, my Harold!" She sagged into the arms of the deputy.

"Well," sighed the attendant, "I guess that's that." He tugged the cover over the body.

Naughton glanced obliquely at Kane. The grizzled sergeant was observing the woman with amused cynicism.

Srack broke the depressing stillness. "This changes the complexion of the case. There is obviously no doubt about the identity of the body found outside. Since the other two were found in bed, the mysterious Mr. Hunt seems to have vanished, if, in fact, he previously existed."

Naughton glared at the lawyer, turned to the sobbing woman.

"I'd like to ask one question, Mrs. Longstreth," he asked. "What is your husband's business, and what was he doing on Hester Street?"

She spoke through her handkerchief.

"Harold was a business man," she gulped. "He made investments and deals like that. I'm ignorant of such things. He went there to visit a Mr. Ritter. They were in some business venture together." She leaned heavily on the deputy's arm. "Please, could you help me to a cab?"

The deputy looked flattered. "Of course, of course," he murmured and took her arm.

Kane suddenly stepped forward.

"Just a minute," he growled. "Maybe I'd like to ask a few questions myself."

The deputy frowned. "But, Sergeant, Mrs. Longstreth—"

Kane gave a brittle laugh.

"Mrs. Longstreth, hell! Stop the dramatics, Tena, and come clean. What was Stoltz doing in the Hester Street house?"

The deputy coroner was flabbergasted. "Stoltz? But I think—"

KANE BARKED at him: "This woman is Tena Stoltz. Her husband is Barney Stoltz, big-time beer baron and one of the worst rats spawned in St. Louis by Prohibition. He is wanted by at least four cities, aside from this one. All right, Tena, what's it all about? Or do I take you down to headquarters?"

Srack held up his hand.

"Your attack on this woman is contemptible!" he snapped at the veteran homicide dick. "Madame, I am a counselor-at-law. May I be of service to you?"

The woman wagged her head, her eyes focused on the hard-bitten features of Kane.

"I don't need a mouthpiece now," she rasped. "Not to deal with a slug-nutty heel like this official tramp. You called it, Kane. I'm Tena Stoltz. I'm not afraid of you for you can't hurt my Barney now."

"Well, that's one good thing about the fire," Kane grunted. "Were the other two guys rats like Barney?"

"Go earn your salary, you big skunk!" Her features warped emotionally, and she burst into a spasm of sobbing.

The little deputy patted her bouncing shoulder and scowled at the sergeant.

"There, there!" he breathed in her ear.

Kane chuckled without mirth. "For a worn-out, burlesque strip-dancer, Tena, you still bowl 'em over."

The deputy colored, led the weeping woman from the room.

Srack squinted at the sergeant. "You're the most ruthless, vicious sadist I've ever seen," he grated. "I demand the release of my client, Mr. Vogel, and I warn you, I'll stand for no fooling around."

Kane glanced at Kovack.

"Kovy, remind me to look up that word he called me, an' if it means something dirty, remind me to kick hell out of this ambulance-chasing shyster."

"Why don't you kick hell outa him first an' then look it up?" the Polack suggested.

Naughton outlined his jaw with his hand.

"I can't understand this—not yet," he mused. "But I don't think we should release Vogel until—"

"You're damn right you won't release him," Kane barked. "This case is just beginning to get interesting. Maybe that third guy is Hunt?"

Naughton wagged his head.

"Not if he was in bed with this Ritter. Hunt didn't have time to get that far into the house. That Stoltz woman—"

"She's a hard character," Kane put in. "Hard as nails. She was in burlesque for nearly twenty years, then, about six years ago she leaped into prominence as the redhead alibi that saved Barney from fryin'. The cops in San Francisco had him cold on a murder rap, but Tena came forward an' claimed he was in a hotel room with her the night of the killin'. He married her as soon as the jury sprung him. Since that time, she's fronted for him in a lot of crooked business. I'm damn glad he's gone, only I wish she'd been with him."

Naughton moved toward the door.

"Dave, have Doctor Phillips telephone me at headquarters as soon as he completes his autopsy." He trudged out to the squad car, the others following.

CHAPTER THREE
TOO MANY TEETH

IT WAS nearly two o'clock by the time the three dicks reached headquarters, after booking Mose Vogel on an open charge of investigation. Kane refused to get excited about the case and seemed satisfied with the arrest of Vogel. Kovack, if he had any opinion of his own, failed to exhibit it. He did, however, complain that he was hungry, so he left his companions at the steps of Central Station and crossed the street to Petie's Dining Car.

"Every time I take Kovy to the morgue," Kane explained. "He gets hungry for ham and eggs. He must be neurotic."

Naughton smiled grimly and led the way to his own cubby-hole. The realization that the body found in the alley was not that of Ralph Hunt left him with a sense of bewilderment. Although there was still one corpse to be identified, reason argued that it could not be the young investigator. Yet, if it were not, what could have happened to the boy? He expressed this uncertainty to the sergeant.

Kane shrugged.

"Maybe this Hunt kid followed Vogel away an' then lost him."

"He would have come back," Naughton reasoned. "His fiancé was waiting in his car on the street."

Kane showed a trace of impatience.

"My job is to apprehend killers, not nurse along a lot of adolescent amateur dicks. This Hunt kid isn't dead, so he ain't no worry of mine." He turned as Kovack came into the room with two sandwiches in his hand and one in his mouth.

"They had some nice crisp pork," the Pole mumbled. "I brung along a couple with pickles."

"The power of suggestion," Kane growled, and waved his partner away.

Naughton started to speak when the phone jangled. He reached for it, listened a moment, then said, "Send him in," and hung up.

"A private dick named Lem Prigge wants to see me about the fire," he told the others. "Know him?'

Kane's furrowed old face hardened.

"Prigge is the shrewdest gum-shoe outside the law," he snorted, "There must be dough tied into this touch-off to bring him into it."

"Maybe Srack sent him," Kovack chirped up. "He did some work for Srack last year." He went back to his second sandwich as the door pushed inward, and a tall, wedge-shaped man barged in.

Prigge stood just inside the door, surveying the trio. His face, under the canted derby, was rectangular and looked as if it might have been chipped out of sandstone. His eyes were small, like bullet holes, but filled with expression. He seemed sardonically amused.

He unbuttoned a Cravenette coat, thumbed back his hat and slumped into a chair,

"Well," he drawled. "You birds look glum enough. I was down to the morgue just after you'd left. I understand you identified two of the three stiffs in that Hester Street explosion. The dumb deputy wouldn't kick through with the names. Who were they?"

Kane and Naughton exchanged glances. The sergeant gave his head an imperceptible shake, so Naughton said: "We're still working on the case, Prigge. Until we learn the identities of all three, we are treating it as confidential matter."

Prigge sniffed.

"I get it. You'd rather split a reward three ways than four. Well, I never come to the cops with a question unless I already got the answer myself. A little bird told me one of those stiffs was the celebrated Barney Stoltz. If that's true, my trail is ended."

"Meanin'?" Kane growled.

"Meanin' that the cops are pretty damn dumb if they don't know who the third stiff is. You've had the information in your records for over a week. That's where I found 'em." He chuckled again, started to get up.

KANE SHOVED him back into a chair. "I hate playin' questions-an'-answers, Prigge. You didn't bust in here to sing that two-bit solo an' go out. What's the gag? Make it plain, because this damn Polack partner of mine had my nerves raw even before you came in."

"Then one of 'em was Stoltz?" Prigge insisted.

Kane nodded impatiently. "What's your interest? And who is this third man?"

"About eight days ago," Prigge told them, "a Mrs. Anselle Hanson reported that her husband had been kidnaped."

"That dentist?" Kane asked.

"That's the one. He was a retired dentist. She brought in two ransom notes and, when you birds couldn't give her any service, she hired me. I got a tip that Barney Stoltz was dabbling in kidnaping, so I came down to your record bureau and checked the writing of the ransom notes with Stoltz's handwriting on his fingerprint card. It checked. For the last six days, I been trying to pick up some trace of Barney Stoltz. Tonight, I got a tip that he was in cahoots with a mugg named Ritter." He shrugged. "I didn't get the news in time to make myself the five grand Mrs. Hanson offered for her husband alive."

Kane whistled discordantly.

"If that's true, then Ritter an' Stoltz were holding this guy Hanson in the Hester Street joint until the dough was paid."

Naughton frowned. "That's a logical hypothesis, but can it be proven?"

"Remind me," Kane called to his partner, "to look up them two four-bit words."

Lem Prigge reached into the inside pocket of his checkered suit, fished out a small, loose-leaf notebook and flipped the pages.

"I got a detailed description of this Hanson," he said. "I'd like to check it with your data on the stiff before I have to tell the little lady that I couldn't earn the five grand because she has become a widow, Here it is: Anselle Hanson was forty-nine years, five feet—"

Kane butted in. "You can't tell much about a loaf of bread from a piece of burnt toast. If this guy was a dentist, perhaps his wife could tell something about his teeth. Stoltz's wife knew about his."

Prigge bobbed his head.

"I got that, too. The upper incisors—"

Naughton reached for the telephone.

"Wait a minute until I get the morgue on the phone. I'll pass it along to them."

Prigge waited until Naughton got his connection, then dictated: "Both upper central incisors covered with gold crowns. Gold inlays in the first and third lower right molars. If they want, I can get the dental chart from Mrs. Hanson. She showed it to me when she gave me this data."

Naughton repeated the information to the attendant and held the line while Dave went off to check with the corpse. However, it was Doctor Phillips, the autopsy surgeon, himself, who came back on the line.

"Hello, Naughton. I was just concluding my autopsy, when Dave brought in your information. It cheeks perfectly. Can you give me the name for my records?"

Naughton told him, and asked if the autopsy had disclosed anything of importance, or evidence of foul play.

"No indication of the sort," Phillips assured him. "Of course the bodies were badly burned, but I found smoke in the lungs of all three which definitely proves they died of asphyxiation."

"Well," Prigge demanded, as Naughton slowly pronged the receiver, "was I right, or was I right?"

Naughton bobbed his head. "Your description tallies. However, I can't understand the motive for arson if the house was used as a hide-away for criminals."

Kane frowned. "Well, it didn't have to be arson. It could have been an accident."

"That's the trouble with you cops," Prigge jeered. "You can't see wood for trees. You, Naughton, get paid to uncover arson, so you can't see anything but fire. Me, now, I haven't got any phobias."

"That makes another word to look up," Kane threw at Kovack.

Prigge smirked and went on: "I follow my nose. I look up this Stoltz guy prove he wrote the notes by checking the police records, and dump the whole solution right in your laps. Now, you mope around and say you don't understand it."

Naughton bit his lip. "You did a smart piece of work when you checked the handwriting," he told Prigge, "but in all your calculations you overlook two factors—Mose Vogel, who owned the house and shows guilty knowledge of the fire—and Ralph Hunt who called me to the scene and told me it was a touch-off."

The private dick chuckled, tilted his chair back and began to smoke.

"There's several ways to explain that," he drawled. "Vogel may have been in the neighborhood, by a coincidence. Naturally, he would run from you when he knew his house was burning. As for this Hunt bird, well, he may have found out that Ritter and Stoltz were holding Hanson there and wanted to cut himself in on the reward, or, as far as that goes, he might have been mixed up with Vogel in the touch-off. These insurance dicks have horned in on the racket before this."

NAUGHTON RESISTED the impulse to smack Prigge. A glance at the two homicide dicks satisfied him that they were in agreement with Lem Prigge, so far as young Hunt was concerned. Despite his confidence in the insurance op, however, Naughton could offer no explanation for his uncanny disappearance.

Prigge took his leave, and after a few futile remarks Kane and Kovack trudged off to their own office. Naughton slumped in his swivel-chair, cocked his hat over his eyes and smoked three cigarettes, one after another. Then he rose, tramped up to the record bureau on the second floor and secured a photograph of Mose Vogel taken at the time of his arrest the year before. Thus armed, he left the station-house and drove to the State Street Emergency Hospital.

IT WAS not until he stood before the registration desk of the hospital that Todd Naughton recalled that he did not know the name of Hunt's fiancée. However, when he displayed his credentials and explained the circumstances, he learned from the orderly that the girl's name was Marian Dolan. He asked to see her at once.

The orderly puckered up his red face in an expression of doubt. "She had a terrific shock," he told the arson dick. "She's sitting in her room, staring at the wall. The doctor said she wasn't to be disturbed."

"Listen," snapped Naughton. "That girl is torturing herself by reliving a scene that never happened. She believes her fiancé was killed before her eyes. Well, it wasn't her man. Now, do you take me to her so I can spare her any further agony, or do I have to barge into every room in this joint until I find her?"

The orderly looked injured. "You cops get so damn tough if you don't get your way about everything. O.K., the responsibility is yours. You'll find her in Room One-two-eight—second door on the left beyond the elevators."

Naughton growled his thanks and strode down the silent corridor. He wondered just what he would say to the girl—just what he could say. He stopped before the door, took off his hat and drummed his fingers on the panel. He waited a moment, then cautiously pushed open the door and eased inside.

Great hurt eyes peered at him from a face made strangely pale by the loss of brows and lashes. She was not crying, not outwardly, but the agony inside showed in every line of her slender body. She rested against piled pillows, long black hair drawn severely off the oval of her face. Her hands lay limp on the covers. Naughton wondered how deeply she was under the influence of opiates.

"I'm Todd Naughton," he told her lamely. "I was at—"

"I know," she said, and her voice seemed to come from a distance. "You carried me away from the fire. I guess I should thank you."

"Miss Dolan, you've suffered one bad jolt tonight. I don't wish to be abrupt, to jar you too much—"

"Please, say it. I'm quite all right now."

Naughton squirmed. He hated to convey news of any kind that affected the emotions of a woman.

"That man—the one you saw blown out of the house. It was not Ralph, He wasn't in the house!"

She moved stiffly out of the pillows, sat erect, staring at him with eyes made large by disbelief. She tried to speak, but her soft, full lips trembled impotently.

"It's true," he insisted, as if she had openly contradicted him. "We have identified the three bodies that were found in the fire. Ralph was not one of them."

Tears welled over the lashless rim of her eyes.

"Then where—where is my Ralph?"

"We don't know that. He has completely disappeared. Now, if you feel strong enough, I need your help."

"Oh, I'll do anything—*anything!*"

Naughton nodded his approval. "Fine! Now, when Ralph met me, he said that he was taking you to the theater when he picked up the trail of the torch—that is, the man who starts fires. Can you tell me who that man was, or anything about him?"

Marian Dolan leaned back against the pillows, but now her whole body was stiff and vibrant with excitement.

"We stopped at a service-station," she explained in a whisper. "Ralph needed gas in his car. Then he drove suddenly out of the station before the attendant could serve us. He was excited. He pointed to a man who, he said, was buying several gallons of naptha cleaning solvent. Ralph explained that he had heard the man in question was tied up in an arson ring of some kind and that it looked like a heaven-sent chance to catch him red-handed. We drove around the block, waited until the man left the station, then followed him to Hester Street. Then, when he went into the house, Ralph hurried over to the drug store to telephone you. You know the rest."

"But the name of the man you followed?"

"Ralph didn't tell me," she admitted.

Naughton fished the photograph of Vogel out of his pocket, bent over and handed it to Marian Dolan.

"Think carefully," be suggested. "Does that look like the man you saw purchasing the naptha?"

She gave her head a decisive shake. "This is not the man. He was younger, harder looking—oh, I can't give you a description for I only had a glance at his face. But I know definitely that this was not the man. He wasn't even the same type."

Naughton sighed, recovered his picture.

"That helps, but negatively," he admitted ruefully. "I can't find a motive for arson, if Vogel is not mixed into it."

"You are really sure about those—those bodies? The identification was quite positive? Ralph couldn't be among—" She stopped to keep back the tears.

His nod was emphatic.

"Unusually positive. Although the bodies were terribly charred, in two cases we had complete data on the teeth. One man was a dentist, and his wife was able to supply the private detective she hired with a dental chart. The wife of the other man—"Naughton paused, his forehead wrinkled.

"Yes," urged the girl. "The other wife was positive also?"

The detective's forehead was corrugated in thought.

"Extremely positive," he growled musefully. "As a matter of fact, she was almost too positive for a woman of her type. A former burlesque hoofer doesn't often know the condition of her man's teeth so accurately that she can describe them in professional language on a moment's notice."

"Did she do that? How strange?"

Naughton pushed himself out of the chair in which he had been seated.

"Are you going to find Ralph?" she asked plaintively.

"I'm going to try mighty hard," he promised her. "You lie there like a good kid. I'll call you as soon as I learn anything."

"God bless you," she called softly. "I'm sorry for what I said at the fire."

He smiled his appreciation, and went out.

CHAPTER FOUR
DEAD MAN ALIVE

DOCTOR PHILLIPS was preparing to leave, when Naughton strode into the morgue and cornered him in his odorous little laboratory. The veteran autopsy surgeon was a gaunt, bald-headed man with shoulders rounded by a score of years spent over the corpses of the city's questionable dead.

"Doc," Naughton opened up bluntly, "there's something phony about this mess. You stated defiantly that all three of the dead died of asphyxiation."

Phillips frowned over his glasses.

"That's what I said."

"But one of those men—the one they identified as Stoltz—was blown out of the building by the explosion. He landed on his head in a cement driveway, crushing the skull. That, mind you, happened a few seconds ahead of the actual fire."

The surgeon shook a bony forefinger.

"Now, listen to me, son," he barked. "I've been at this business a long time. If a man crushes his skull, he's dead. No doubt about that. And if he's dead, he don't breathe. Well, those three dead men breathed during the fire because they had smoke in their lungs. I don't care what you think you saw!"

"Is there any way the smoke might have filtered into the lungs after death?"

"Impossible! The lungs are like bellows, and smoke would have to be pumped or sucked into them by the physical action of a living body. Smoke cannot enter by any other means. Impossible, sir!"

NAUGHTON SCOWLED, lighted a cigarette. He was standing on the threshold of an important discovery, but the secret was veiled and he couldn't find the key to pass it. He took a slow turn around the stuffy lab. His unseeing eyes flitted over the grisly objects in sealed jars. Spotted lungs, diseased brains, body organs in varying conditions—the results of Phillips' constant investigations and experiments, and the reasons why he was accredited the smartest autopsy surgeon in the state.

And, despite all this, Todd Naughton could not accept the verdict of the veteran surgeon. He had seen the body strike the pavement, and life must have passed at that moment, if not before.

"Just what are you driving at?" Phillips demanded truculently.

Naughton turned, leaned against a specimen-case.

"It doesn't check," he told the other. "You say all three died of smoke, yet I saw one man killed before there was any smoke. I saw that with my own eyes."

"What else?"

Naughton stroked his chin. "Well, it may have no significance, but Tena Stoltz was pretty well armed with the technical condition of her husband's teeth."

"Well, what do you make from that?"

"Stoltz was dead before the fire started. He might have been dead even before the explosion."

Phillips sighed.

"But damn it, sir!" he shouted in exasperation. "Are you doubting my word, when I tell you I found smoke in his lungs?"

Naughton shook his head. "No, I'm trying to find the answer, that's all. You say those lungs are like bellows. Now, isn't it a fact that they pump the water out of the lungs of a man who has drowned? Isn't it possible, by artificial respiration, to stimulate the bellows action of the lungs and suck smoke into them?"

Phillips glared at the dick, then walked around his desk and sat down. He fixed his eyes on a small calendar, his long, tapering fingers toying with a small scalpel.

"It's fantastic, sir, positively fantastic!" he muttered after a long pause. "Yet, what you describe is possible. Yes, if a cadaver were bent over a barrel, let us say, and a smudge-pot, or some other kind of fire kindled in such a manner that the smoke would envelop the head, that smoke could be sucked into the dead lungs by rolling the body, as in artificial respiration. If that were done, then of course an autopsy would be deceptive."

"Exactly!" snapped the arson dick. "And Barney Stoltz may have been dead, the smoke pumped into his lungs as you suggest, and the house on Hester Street blown up deliberately to make it appear that Stoltz had died in the fire, instead of by other means."

THE OLD surgeon nodded wearily. "Possible, yes—possible. Though I shudder to think of all the autopsies which have been performed, and decisive decisions rendered, because smoke was found in the lungs." He sighed again. "But why would anyone go to that much trouble to disguise the real cause of death in a wanted criminal? The police would be delighted to find Barney Stoltz dead by any means,"

"That," Naughton growled, "is precisely what I intend to find out. Now, about this Stoltz woman—did she leave an address with you or arrange for the disposal of the body?"

"She didn't give me an address, but she left a telephone number and asked me to call the minute she could claim the body. She wants to go back to her folks in St. Louis. At first she intended to take the body with her and asked if an undertaker could rebuild Stoltz's features so his relatives could see him. When I assured her that was impossible, she spoke of having the cadaver disposed of here. She seems anxious to get away and"—Phillips permitted himself a dry smile—"she hates cops."

"Have you called her?"

"Not yet. I telephoned Sergeant Kane a few minutes ago and he said to let her have the body, said he didn't even want Stoltz buried in this town. I was just I about to call her when you blew in. Of course, we shan't release the body, with events as they have developed."

"On the contrary, we shall let her have it," Naughton countered, "although we may take it away from her again. Where is the telephone number she gave you?"

Phillips leaned over a memo pad on his littered desk.

"She continued using the name of Longstreth. The number is Federal Six-two-one-o-three. That would be in the Wilshire District."

Naughton went over to the phone, called the special agent of the telephone company, and requested the location of Federal 6-2103.

"Not a bad guess," he admitted, on hanging up. "It's in Suite Six Hundred and Seventy-eight of the Valerie Apartments on Circle Drive. Funny how criminals like this Stoltz will hibernate in a respectable district."

"A subconscious desire to be decent," Phillips observed. "What do you expect to gain by letting her have the body of her husband?"

Naughton glanced at his watch.

"I'd like a chance to search her apartment. If I can find out why they pumped smoke into Barney Stoltz's lungs after he died, or was killed, I'll find out who is behind the plot. When I learn that, I'll find the answer to the disappearance of young Hunt."

"The sergeant thinks Hunt took a runout on the case."

"That sergeant," growled Naughton, "gets ants in his pants. Now, here's what you do. Give me twenty minutes to get out to the Valerie Apartments, then you call Tena Stoltz. Tell her, if she is anxious to have the body, she can claim it at once if she will come down and sign a release while you are here, otherwise she will have to wait until tomorrow afternoon. It's my guess she'll come immediately, if she's as anxious as you suggested."

"And you?"

Naughton swung around, picked up the phone and called headquarters. He asked for Sergeant Kane, but the doughty homicide dick was out, so Naughton left his name and hung up.

"I'm going to the Valerie," he answered Phillips' previous query. "Try to find out what she intends doing with Barney's body. Also, make a note of the conveyance that carts it away. We may want to trace it if anything develops,"

"What will I tell Kane if he calls back?"

Naughton paused as he went through the doorway.

"Tell him to feed that Polish echo," he grinned.

IT WAS cold and bleak, and the dawn was less than an hour away, as Naughton hunched in the black chasm of shadow between two stone buildings, his eyes haunting the barred front door of the Valerie. He shifted his weight from one foot to the other, in a vain effort to keep warm, and kept glancing at the luminous dial of his wrist-watch. Fifty minutes had already passed since he left the morgue, yet the Stoltz woman had not appeared. Suppose she left the corpse in the care of the authorities? A husband wasn't much good when he was merely a charred cadaver.

He tried to keep his mind off Ralph Hunt. He must, he warned himself, proceed by a set routine, of which emotion could not play a part. Yet, it was almost impossible to maintain a detached perspective for he felt a disturbing responsibility for the young operative's disappearance.

The sudden arrival of a taxi before the Valerie disbanded his musing. As it slowed to a stop, Tena Stoltz darted out of the apartment building and entered the tonneau. The cab swung into motion. Naughton stepped out of hiding, jotted down the license number of the hack, and watched the red blob of taillight swallowed in the haze of darkness. He waited another three or four minutes, then out diagonally across the street to the apartment house.

The big front door was not locked, so he passed into the dim-lit lobby. He encountered no one, and, avoiding the elevators, ducked up the deep-carpeted stairs.

Tiny globules of perspiration beaded his face as he leveled off on the sixth floor and located Number 678, a front apartment. He stooped over, looking for a slash of light beneath the door. There was none. He punched the bell, put his ear to the panel. He heard the buzzer inside, but no one answered.

Naughton grinned his satisfaction. With a long triggerfinger, he gaffed a ring of master keys out of his vest pocket. The lock on the door surrendered to his fourth effort, and he silently pushed inside.

He closed the door softly, his back against it. The apartment was dark, save for two large, rectangular patches that were windows. He inched toward them, feeling his way like a blind man, then drew the shades and groped back to the light-switch near the door. He made sure the door was locked, pressed the switch, and the details of the big room magically evolved out of the darkness.

Naughton blinked, then stared. A feeling of emptiness raided his stomach; his hackles crawled erect. He brought his hands up, slowly.

There were two men in the room, one on either side of it They leaned casually over the backs of two chairs, their guns pointed at the arson dick. Naughton recognized them instantly, yet, somehow, his mind refused to accept the amazing declaration of his eyes. For one of the men was Lem Prigge, the other—Todd Naughton blinked again.

The second man was Barney Stoltz!

"We saw you cross the street," Prigge remarked with a twisted smirk. "We sort of figured you'd come up."

The sarcastic twang of the private dick's voice whipped Naughton back to reality, but his brain still stumbled over the unexpected turn of events. He felt his eyes drawn again to Barney Stoltz, and they hardened as he realized the criminal was very much alive.

"Well," Naughton growled, "you guys are full of surprises."

Prigge chuckled. "Cops are always surprised when they run into something they can't understand, which is most of the time." He moved closer. "I'll just trouble you for that gun before you get absent-minded." He slid an experienced hand to Naughton's holster, removed the gun.

Stoltz impaled Naughton with boarish little red-flecked eyes. He was a big man, though not so tall as Prigge or Naughton, but heavier for he was built close to the ground. His face was flat, like a slab of cement and he had a fire-brick complexion. His ordinarily bald plate was bushed over by an auburn-hued wig that altered his appearance considerably.

"Why'd you come here? he demanded, and his voice had that peculiarly grating quality of a wild beast, snarling over a chunk of meat.

NAUGHTON HESITATED. He knew he was in the tightest spot of his career, and that if he escaped alive it would be by wit alone. Both Prigge and Stoltz were shrewd, cunning, as timber wolves are shrewd and cunning. They were desperate. Stoltz was already a fugitive with a price on his head, and now it was obvious that Prigge was in with him.

"Your racket blew up," the arson dick said slowly, feeling his way with caution. "We discovered that the body identified as you did not die in the Hester Street fire."

"Who's 'we?'" Stoltz snarled.

Naughton managed a smile of contempt.

"That's something you'll find out in one hell of a hurry!"

A trapped look flooded the little shoe-button eyes of the hunted man, and for a moment Naughton was afraid he would shoot. It was Prigge who relieved the tension, to the relief of the arson dick.

"He's bluffing, Barney," Prigge chuckled. "I called that dumb old flat-foot, Kane, a few minutes ago and asked him when Mrs. Hanson could have the other body. Kane is still pushing around this stooge, Vogel. He doesn't care what happens to the stiffs."

"How'd this gum-shoe get here?" Stoltz reiterated.

Prigge shrugged. "He's still worrying about that damned insurance op. We ran into a bit of tough luck when that stiff went through the roof. Between those two mishaps, this guy got an idea—and here he is."

Stoltz glared coldly at the prisoner.

"It was your damn dumbness in letting that gum-shoe follow you to the house in the first place!" he barked at Prigge. "You should have caved in his skull and chucked him into the place instead of carting him away. You didn't use your head."

Naughton felt a sudden surge of elation. So Prigge was the man whom Ralph tailed from the gas station. It was Prigge that torched the Hester Street house; by the same token, Prigge had taken the young dick away some place. With that realization, Naughton's hopes collapsed. They would have done away with the boy by this time.

"Don't be a damn fool," Prigge jeered. "How in hell could I stop to monkey around with that mugg when I knew the house was due to go up in a couple of minutes? If I'd left him there they would have known it was a touch-off. Now, they're only guessing."

Stoltz shifted his grip on the gun butt.

"We better pick up Tena an' scram."

"Take it easy," Prigge drawled. "This is the only guy who is wise you're alive, and we can handle him. Don't worry about Tena. They haven't got a damn thing on her, so we'll wait until she calls back like she planned. If she don't call, we'll slide out to the hide-away until I can look around. Tena can take care of herself. She's a better actress off stage than on. Why, Barney, she nearly had those dumb flatties in tears when she threw her act in the morgue. Now, if only that dumb Kane—"

"I wish we had Kane here with this monkey." Stoltz rasped.

Lem Prigge chuckled, and the sound sent a chill rippling up Naughton's spine. Prigge backed him into the divan, then perched atop the table, one leg dangling. Stoltz crouched back of his chair, like a sputtering fuse. A brooding silence claimed them.

Naughton was just as well satisfied for the conversation had crowded his mind with more information that he could readily digest. He was, he knew, with his back to the wall, figuratively and literally. Stoltz, hunched across the room, itched to kill him. Stoltz' antagonism was motivated by hate and fear. Yet it was in Lem Prigge that Naughton recognized his most dangerous opponent. Ever cool, shrewd and calculating, the sardonic Prigge would be a most difficult man to outwit.

IT WAS logical that Stoltz should be alive—it gave reason to the action of Tena, explained the purpose of the dead man who had smoke pumped into his lungs after he was dead. Yet, Naughton found it hard to hold this truth, even with the fugitive before him. It opened so many new channels, so many unanswered questions. If this were Stoltz, as admittedly it was, then who was the man who had been blown through the wall of the house on Hester Street? And what of the other two corpses? Were they phonies, too? And where did these corpses come from?

The phone jangled, and Prigge leaned back across the table, scooped the bulb from the prong.

"Hello," he mumbled, then after a pause his voice resumed its natural twang and he asked: "Where are you calling from?… O.K., now get this—make sure you haven't picked up a tail, then fan out to Bilsky's. Go in the back way. If you get there before us, tell Bilsky to fire up. The stiffs have to be disposed of tonight…. Yeah, we had a guest; we're bringin' him along." He forked the receiver, pushed erect.

"Like shootin' fish in a rain-barrel," he told the scowling Stoltz. "Tena got the stiff and stuck around until Oscar carted it away, then she called from a hash-house across from the morgue. So you've got nothing to worry about, Barney, because you're officially dead. Isn't that right, Naughton?"

"I wouldn't know," the arson dick growled. "A well-placed slug would make him a lot deader."

"Why, you—" Snarled Stoltz and shifted his gun.

"Cut it!" barked Prigge. "He's only goading you to start something here in the apartment. Wait until—" His frown melted into a meaning smirk. "I better shackle him meanwhile." He took a pair of cuffs and joined Naughton's wrists.

"I'll wait," Stoltz jerked. "But not long. Let's get out of here."

Prigge nodded, crossed to the door. He moved easily, gliding along on the balls of his feet; he reminded Naughton of a well-conditioned panther.

"I'll take a look around," Prigge suggested. "Wait here."

He eased into the corridor, softly closed the door. Alone with Stoltz, Naughton gauged his chances of making a break. They seemed hopeless. The gunman stood braced behind a substantial chair. He could empty his gun before the arson dick could even move from the soft, clinging depths of the divan. Naughton was still thinking about it when Prigge reentered the apartment.

"All clear," he told them. "The car is in the alley." He fixed Naughton with a cold stare. "You're probably thinking of escape, but forget it. You make a break here, and we'll crack your spine. Besides that, some innocent people would probably get shot up."

"That," jeered Naughton, "would worry hell out of you."

Stoltz moved up behind him, pistol-whipped him over the head.

"Shut up, cop, an' get movin'!"

Groggy, and a little nauseated, Todd Naughton stumbled down the six long flights in the wake of the lithe

Prigge. Like three weary ghosts they flitted across a darkened alley, thence into a closed sedan. Lem Prigge was at the wheel when the machine tooled out of the shadows and raced west, as though running away from the filtering rays of dawn.

CHAPTER FIVE
OVENS FOR THE DEAD

NAUGHTON DIDN'T try to think much during the ride. Instead, he slumped low in the seat beside Stoltz and gave his aching head a chance to clear. The big car poured through the deserted street and, about a mile out of town, swung onto a county road for several miles. Naughton had a vague premonition of their destination, but refused to think about it. After a while, the sedan turned into a tree-fringed dirt road. A ruddy splash in the eastern sky began to lengthen the shadows of the trees, and, when the machine slowed for its final turn, Naughton saw the journey's end.

Hunched down in the middle of a straggling graveyard, the domed roof of the crematory resembled a gigantic beehive. Prigge slowed, shifted to second and threaded the sedan between the rows of marble headstones, now ghostly in the half light of morning.

"This place," Stoltz growled, "gives me the jeebies."

Prigge laughed without much humor, brought the sedan to a stop behind the crematory. Simultaneously, a door opened and a shriveled figure paused silhouetted in the frame, staring at them.

"O.K.," Prigge called. "It's us, Oscar. Where's Bilsky?"

The man called Oscar moved toward the car. A deformity in one leg gave him an unnatural gait, and he approached at an angle with the strange, sidewise motion of a crab crossing a wet rock.

"The woman," Oscar croaked in a hushed tone, as if he were reading a funeral service, "she came just a minute ago. Bilsky is starting the blowers." He glimpsed Naughton hunched beside Stoltz. "Who is that?"

Prigge chuckled, shunted his long frame to the ground and tugged open the rear door.

"Another guest," he told the cripple. Oscar peered at the arson dick, and his little round eyes were appraising.

"The other one," he told Prigge, "is still in the storage vault. You want to put this one there?"

Prigge shot an oblique glance at Stoltz. A question and its inevitable answer passed between them.

"No," Prigge said at last. "There isn't time. This one is—"

"A cop," hissed Oscar. "I knew it! I knew it the minute I laid my eyes on him. A cop!"

As they moved toward the crematory, another man loomed in the doorway, etched by the lighted room beyond.

"Oscar!" he called. "Who is it, Oscar?"

"It's them," Oscar cackled. "It's them, an' they brought a cop with them!"

The man in the opening backed away to let them pass. Naughton gave him a sharp glance. He was gangling, loose-jointed, with a hairless head and sunken cheeks, as if he had perhaps stepped from one of the graves outside.

He closed the door as soon as they were inside.

"I don't like it," he whined. "I didn't bargain for this. Another one? When is it going to end?"

Stoltz started to speak, but Prigge silenced him with a gesture.

"It couldn't be helped, Bilsky," the private dick explained placatingly. "This guy stumbled onto the trick, so we got to protect ourselves."

"I don't like it," the cadaverous-faced man reiterated. "I didn't bargain on murder."

"You went into this with your eyes open," Stoltz bit at him, "an' you got damn well paid for your end of it. Well, you'll get paid for these two more."

"But murder!" whined the old man. "It'll be murder."

Stoltz uttered a short, bark-like laugh.

"This is gonna be my treat," he snarled. "It won't concern you."

"That's a damned lie," Naughton put in. "They hang you for joining in a murder conspiracy, Bilsky, and—"

STOLTZ HIT him a backhand swipe that knocked him over a rectangular pine box laying on the floor. As Naughton stumbled to his feet; Stoltz rammed the end of a revolver against his chest.

Once again it was Lem Prigge who interfered… and saved the arson dick's life.

"Hold it, Barney," Prigge snapped, in that strangely commanding tone. "Wait until we get the other one up here. That's why I didn't knock him off sooner. We only wanted to do the job once, and do it thoroughly." He turned to the cripple. "Oscar, you and Barney bring up the insurance op. Bilsky, where is Tena?"

The old man canted his head toward a metal-covered sliding door.

"Inside," he jerked, and moved ahead of them.

Prigge gestured with the muzzle of his revolver.

"O.K., Naughton. Walk ahead of me."

Naughton followed the cadaverous Bilsky through the fire-proof door. His head ached from the blows he had received and a whirring noise, like wind howling through a tunnel, seemed to pervade everything. Only when he entered the long vault containing the four cremating-ovens, did he realize that the noise came from the powerful blowers which forced the oil into the white-hot furnaces.

The place was dim-lit, but, from each of the ovens, a yellow torch of light escaped through peep-holes in the door. It licked up the walls, danced across the low ceiling and peered into the faces of the silent men, as if perhaps it were a living organism wondering which of there was going to enter that dissolving, man-made hell.

Tena was crouched against the wall, surveying the scene with a sadistic expression on her face. Her full breasts rose and fell rhythmically, and her eyes caught and held some of the feverish intensity of the flames. The momentary jabs of light were not kind to her worn features, and tiny globules of perspiration beaded through the crust of powder.

Bilsky crossed to a smaller door between the ovens. He shielded his face with a bony hand, opened a small door, He closed it hastily, turned.

"It takes about fifteen minutes to get them hot enough," he whispered. "I don't like it, I tell you."

Naughton tore his eyes from the great ovens.

"Prigge," he said, striving to keep his voice on a casual level, "You should know you can't get away with wholesale murder of this kind. You'll hang and you'll take all these others with you."

"We haven't killed anybody yet," Bilsky whined to Prigge. "Can't we keep 'em prisoners or something until we clean up big? Then we can beat it where they won't find us. I'm afraid of murder."

Lem Prigge smiled. A sudden tongue of light caught his face from below and gave it a satanic cast.

"Naughton, we got the greatest racket in the world; we stand to clean up millions. You and this Hunt lad stumbled onto just enough to ruin our plans—if you had lived to tell about it. You've been around enough to see that."

Tena spoke from the shadows. "You talk too much!"

Naughton whipped his head around as a door opened and Ralph Hunt strode into the room in front of Stoltz and the crab-like Oscar.

Hunt's hands were tied behind him. He still wore his sloppy trench-coat, but his hat was gone and his curly brown hair hung loosely over his forehead. His jaw was thrust forward aggressively, but his scowl vanished into a troubled smile at sight of the arson dick.

"Well, Naughton, so these ghouls nabbed you too, eh?" he observed cynically.

Stoltz shoved the young op ahead of him.

"Kiss an' get it over with," he jeered.

There followed a long moment of silence broken only by the sibilant hiss of the oil-blowers.

"For God's sake!" bleated Tena Stoltz. "Do something. That hellish noise gets on my nerves!"

"The fire," Bilsky muttered, "the fire has to be awfully hot!"

Stoltz, too, was impressed by the unholy atmosphere of the hungry hiss of the ovens for cooking the dead. Under the shifting light, his features were contorted and sweaty with emotion.

"Tena's right!" he growled. "Let's get it over with."

NAUGHTON TOOK a quick survey of his chances. They looked remote, yet he seized about for some slight straw. There was, he decided, no sense to die without a fight. If they wanted to kill him, let them earn the right. Stoltz and Prigge were both armed, and holding their guns for immediate action. Tena, too, was probably armed, but now her white-gloved hands gripped the edge of a hand-rail. The man, Oscar, had the powerful compensatory arms of a cripple, and he would have to be reckoned in a rough-and-tumble fight. Old Bilsky, Naughton hazarded, would not count. Hunt's arms were tied and thus nullified much support from that direction.

Prigge asked: "Where's the stiff Oscar brought from the morgue?"

Bilsky pointed to a long pine box near the door.

"There," he croaked. "There's the corpse that caused all the trouble."

"When that goes up," Prigge laughed, "there won't be any more Barney Stoltz. You're practically born again, Barney."

"You're sure there won't be any evidence left?" Tena whispered hoarsely.

Bilsky shook his head and for the first time a touch of pride, of confidence, crept into his tone.

"Nothing," he promised, "will be left but a few bone ashes. The casket and the flesh is burned to nothing and swept away by the blower to dissolve in pure heat. The bones are full of calcium and heavier. We sweep those out and give them to you in an urn."

Tena shuddered. "I don't want 'em!"

"What?" jeered Prigge. "Don't you want the ashes of your loving husband?"

"I'll take the living ashes," the woman panted.

Prigge laughed. "How's that fire, Bilsky? Barney's getting jittery."

Bilsky opened the massive door of the nearest furnace, and Naughton was able to see into the brick oven. A channel ran down the center of the interior, a canal of white-hot flame. The heat drove them back a step.

"The pine box, Oscar!" called the old man. "We will start with the bogus Mr. Stoltz."

As the cripple crept spiderwise along the room, Barney Stoltz moved to the mouth of the roaring oven, peered inside as if drawn by a terrible fascination. He glanced back over his shoulder once at Naughton.

"You'll be in there in a minute, copper," he grated. "I'm going to watch you dissolve!" He turned to the flame.

Oscar scraped the heavy box along the floor, and it rasped like a file drawn across steel.

Naughton knew it was now or never. He tried to catch Hunt's eye, but the young insurance op was staring into the blazing fury of the oven. The light painted them in harsh blacks and whites, and the hiss of the blower, and the scrape of the pine box across the cement floor, put the final touch of horror to the scene.

Naughton watched Prigge. The instant the private dick's eyes wavered, the arson dick acted....

He lunged forward in a long kick. His foot caught Stoltz squarely, catapulted him into the white hell of the oven. Then he threw himself on Prigge.

He heard the insane shrieks of the woman as he crashed into the big private dick. She had Stoltz by one wrist, was trying vainly to pull him from the oven but he sank even as she fought to save him.

Now Todd fought for a grip on Lem Prigge's throat, but the handcuffs hampered him. Prigge, strong, cunning, used the shackled arms as a lever to pry the hands away from his throat.

Naughton struggled to his knees, glimpsed Hunt floundering impotently in the grip of Oscar. He threw down his hand for an instant to catch his balance, and at that moment Prigge dove forward, sent the top of his head crashing into Naughton's face.

The arson dick fought to retain his senses as he toppled backward to the floor. Through blinded eyes, he caught a picture of Prigge swaying erect, a revolver in his hand. Then the agony of his nose made him blink his eyes shut....

A GUN roared! Naughton ducked instinctively. He heard a scream and wondered if Prigge had shot at Hunt. He forced his eyes open in time to see Prigge pirouette, then slowly revolve to the floor. Shadows flittered in front of the open oven, struggling silhouettes of black and white, grotesque forms that wailed and screamed until Naughton was sure his mind had cracked.

Then silence came with startling abruptness, complete silence save for the hissing whirr of the blowers. It was broken when a dry, rough voice growled: "Come on, you! How in hell do you douse these damn ovens?" And Todd Naughton was sure he was moving in a dream.

Yet, when he opened his eyes again, the scene was very real. Sergeant Kane was holding old man Bilsky by the scruff of the neck while the latter turned off the electric blowers.

"I didn't kill nobody," Bilsky was droning, "I never killed anybody."

"We'll talk about that later," Kane promised, and dragged the old mart toward Naughton.

"Hey, Naughton!" Kane called. "Are you all right, boy?"

Naughton turned over, crawled to his hands and knees. He shook his head like a tired pony.

"Hunt," he groaned. "How's Ralph Hunt?"

"O.K.," called the insurance op from across the room. Kane pushed Bilsky into a corner, reached over and assisted Naughton to his feet. A steady pounding seemed to shake the building.

"What in thunder is that?"

Kane grinned. "That's Kovy," he explained. "He wants to get in. Hey, you old Kromo"—this spoken to Bilsky—"open that door an' let my partner in. Don't try to get away—he shoots quick."

NAUGHTON'S HEAD was clearing. He looked around the heat-filled chamber. Prigge was twisted on the floor. Ralph Hunt sat on the edge of the open pine box, grinned. The crippled Oscar lay at his feet, quivering, and across the ribbon of carpet, leading up to the center oven, was stretched the still form of Tena Stoltz.

"She ain't hurt," Kane anticipated his query. "I had to smack her to keep her from diving into the oven."

"Barney Stoltz went in there," Naughton mumbled. "Where'd you come from?"

Kane grunted. "Me? Ah, I was in the pine box. That's the way with you youngsters, you don't give an old-timer credit for anything. When I came back to the morgue an' learned from the doc that you had found something phony about the bodies, an' that Tena here was coming to claim one of 'em, well, I just got sort of curious, as you might say, an' climbed into the pine box just to see what she meant to do with it. I'm gonna bat that damned Oscar another konk on the skull for the rough ride he gimme comin' down here."

A door slammed, and Kovack came striding into the room.

"Say, Sarge," the Pole grumbled, "I had a hell of a time tailin' that dame. She musta been suspicious or something."

"Well, it's not important," Kane snapped at him, "You drag in after the party's over. Now, if I ain't too inquisitive, Naughton, if that stiff I substituted for in the pine box wasn't Barney Stoltz—just who was he? Who killed him?"

"That is one thing," Naughton admitted, "that I wasn't able to figure out."

"He wasn't killed!" Bilsky bleated.

Kane turned on him. "I get it," he snarled sarcastically. "He was just disguised in those charred things to look like he was dead, eh?"

Ralph Hunt interrupted.

"I can explain it, Sergeant. Those three corpses found in the Hester Street fire were dead *before* the explosion, but they were not murdered. You see, this is all part of an elaborate plot. They were the bodies of men who had, in the regular course of business, been brought here to Bilskys mausoleum for cremation.

Prigge needed corpses for his scheme but he knew that if he murdered people, sooner or later there would be a squawk. But by purchasing bodies of people already legally certified as dead, he ran little risk. Instead of burning them as he was supposed to, Bilsky burned up a few old beef bones to give to the bereaved, and sold the bodies to Prigge."

KANE SCOWLED. "Yeah, well I heard Prigge braggin' that he had an idea worth millions, but that still don't answer the thing. How about Vogel? It was his house, an' he certainly acted guilty enough. Then, too, how do you explain the identification of the teeth by Tena Stoltz and the Hanson woman?"

"That was easy," Hunt reasoned. "Prigge is familiar with Srack and his clients. Prigge chose that house on Hester Street because it belonged to Vogel, and he figured that Vogel would be suspected right away because of his past record. Then, as soon as Prigge touched off the house, he called Vogel on the telephone to draw him to the neighborhood. It was a cinch some cop would pick him up."

"We picked him up, all right," Naughton admitted glumly.

"As for the teeth identification by the women," Hunt continued, "they simply made charts of the dental work on the teeth of the cadaver they bought from Bilsky here. This was the first in a long series of such mysteries. Then Prigge arranged with Hanson to frame his death."

"Then Hanson is *alive?*" Kane demanded.

Hunt nodded. "Both Hanson and Ritter. Bilsky can supply the details for he was in with Prigge. Hanson's wife was in it, too, to milch the insurance companies, but Ritter wanted an out so he could get away from his wife and skip out with his secretary. He paid Prigge ten thousand bucks to frame him dead. Prigge discovered the trick of pumping smoke into the lungs of a corpse so as to pass an autopsy, and he realized its potentialities. By getting corpses from Bilsky, he could arrange for the legal disappearance of hunted criminals and any man who wanted to escape his living identity. He could supply ashes of the living and milk the insurance companies out of millions. I stumbled onto Prigge—"

"Marian told me about that," Naughton cut in. "She's half dead from worry, kid, so you better get on a phone. Ask her to marry you right away while she's in the notion.

If she has time to think, she'll never marry a guy in our work—so beat it. I'll explain the rest."

Kovack stirred restlessly.

"Listen," he moaned, "don't you muggs ever eat? It's daylight already, an' I been trampin' through that damned marble orchard outside for the last hour, lookin' for this human incinerator. An' that reminds me—how I could go for a nice barbecued pork san'wich!"

4-ALARM MURDER

TWO MEN—VETERAN SMOKE-EATER AND PAROLED EX-CON—HAD BEEN GUNNED OUT, AND AN ENTIRE BUILDING KINDLED FOR A PYRE TO DEVOUR THEIR LEAD-SIEVED BODIES. THEN ONE HOLOCAUST AFTER ANOTHER FOLLOWED WHILE THE ARSON-DEVIL'S UNHOLY LAUGHTER ECHOED ABOVE THE BLAZE WHICH LICKED AWAY, WITH SCARLET TONGUES, ALL CLUES TO HIS MOTIVES OR IDENTITY.

CHAPTER ONE
WHY BURN THE SLAIN?

CAPTAIN WYATT HAGERDON, veteran skipper of Rescue Company 23, was loafing by the joker-stand when Todd Naughton came into the station house. The arson dick's face was soured. He made no bones about showing it, either. Hagerdon pinged an amber stream of tobacco juice against the polished rim of a cuspidor and said: "You look like something don't agree with you, fella. Your best girl run out on you?"

Naughton grinned. Already he began to feel better. There had been a bad string of incendiary fires during the past months and he had failed to turn up anything worth while and the Old Man had inferred very bluntly that it was a case of turn in the guy-with-the-matches—or turn in the badge. Tonight, he needed the counsel of a veteran, and Wyatt Hagerdon was the shrewdest, toughest smoke-eater who ever shoved his gray thatch into a white-fronted helmet.

"Cap, this series has got me down. I'm whirling in circles and now I'm not sure but maybe the whole business is not just an act of God."

Hagerdon grunted, tested his aim at the shining cuspidor. Since the work of a rescue company, aside from routine duty on actual fires, involves accidents, attempted suicides and murder, it turns up a lot of priceless information and no police detail is more closely related to it than the arson squad, unless, perhaps, the homicide crew.

"No, it's the work of a torch, all right," the skipper mused finally. "They have been far too uniformly successful to be either accidents or the work of a pyromaniac."

Naughton nodded. "Yeah, I know but—" He paused as the telephone gong clanged three times.

"That's mine!" Hagerdon said, jerking off the running-board and diving for a booth. He reappeared in a couple of moments and ran for a closet. "A suicide," he called. "Just

"So help me, mister, I'll kill you
before I let you call the cops!"

a quick run—make it with me." He yanked a large resuscitator case out of the closet and heaved it into the roadster.

Naughton swung into the seat, saying: "O.K., let her roll!"

Hagerdon started the engine and the siren at the same time, and conversation was impossible. The red roadster roared out of the station house, wheeled around a stalled street car and zoomed north along the left hand side of the street. Twelve blocks and Hagerdon tooled it squealing around a bend and wailed west. Five minutes later, he cut off the siren and went into a long, dry skid that butted him into the curb in front of a cheap, four-storied rooming-house. Before the roadster actually stopped rolling, Hagerdon was running across the narrow lawn, the clumsy case banging against his long legs. Naughton sprang to the ground and followed.

HAGERDON OPENED the front door and charged into the small hallway. In the dim, uncertain light of the house, a woman could be seen at the top of the stairs.

"Oh, you were so long—so long!" she moaned. She stood braced against the balustrade, swaying like a tree in the wind.

Hagerdon grunted, and replied by running up the stairs. As he neared the second floor, he demanded: "What's the trouble?"

The woman sobbed, pirouetted and fled up another long, narrow flight. Hagerdon glanced over his shoulder at Naughton and wrinkled his nose. The arson dick sniffed, caught the odor of cooking-gas, then he hurried after the other pair. On the third floor, the woman stopped before a closed door, turned and leaned weakly against the frame.

"He's in there!" she rasped, and added a little moan of despair as her knees buckled and she slid along the wall to the floor.

Hagerdon wasted no time on the woman. He dropped the case, tried the door and found it locked. He stepped back a pace, sized up the strength of the panel, then said over his shoulder to Naughton: *"Gas!* Careful!"

He hit the door with his shoulder, just above the flimsy lock. The door gave, banged crazily on its hinges. Hagerdon slapped a handkerchief over his nose and charged inside.

Naughton caught the treacherous fumes, covered his own nostrils with linen and followed inside, closing the door. He glimpsed the skipper forcing open a large window, so he made for another and opened it as well. Pausing at the opening long enough to exchange old breath for new, he swung around and a low whistle of astonishment escaped him.

The room was a kitchen. A cheap table was placed up close to the large, old-fashioned gas cook-stove, and the body of a man in shirt sleeves lay on the table, his head out of sight in the open oven of the stove.

"Turn—off—gas!" Hagerdon choked out, as he started to pick up the inert body in his arms.

Naughton bobbed his head, bent swiftly and closed the three open jets, then ran across the room and opened the hall door, as Hagerdon staggered out with his limp burden. Once in the corridor, Naughton closed the door to keep the fumes from flooding the rest of the house.

"Where can I lay him down in a bed?" Hagerdon asked the woman.

She reached over, caught the railing of the stairs and pulled herself erect.

"Is he—gone?" she whimpered.

Hagerdon shrugged. "I don't know yet. Don't waste time. Where are your rooms?"

She nodded toward an upward flight. "His room is on the fourth—at the head of the stairs."

Naughton put out his arms to help the fireman, but Hagerdon shook his head. "He's not heavy. You bring that resuscitator." He swung around and stalked toward the upward flight of stairs. The woman stood weakly against the wall, and watched them go up.

They entered a tiny bedroom with sloping eaves and one small, oval window. Hagerdon stumbled across a threadbare carpet and dropped his burden onto a saggy double-bed which squeaked protestingly as the weight struck it. Naughton pulled an old trunk close to the bed and set the case on it. As the fireman began to open his apparatus, the arson dick moved the solitary droplight closer to the bed. Then he got his first good look at the inert man.

The latter was not over five feet three or four, and slight. Because he was bald and the wispy wreath of hair that did fringe his head was gray, his age was uncertain. He was probably in his late forties, however, for his face was deep-furrowed and overcast with a worn, grayish pallor. There was no tremor of movement in the sunken chest.

"Oh, God!" whimpered the woman, from the doorway. "Oh, God—he's dead now!"

Naughton turned his head. She was youngish, about thirty, perhaps, although her eyes were ageless. Her right hand was pressed over her face like a taloned claw, muffling her moans and distorting her features. Her hair was so dark as to seem black and her shapely figure was covered with a cheap dress. One eye was swollen shut, as from a blow, and, on the tip of her nose, was a dark stain that suggested blood. She came into the room and closed the door.

HAGERDON OPENED the case, exposing three tall, metal tanks. He put a rubber-edged cone over the nose and mouth of the man on the bed and turned a valve. At once the machine began to function. A small rubber lung, like a football bladder, which was connected to the front of the resuscitator, started to fill and empty as the mixture of oxygen and carbon dioxide was pumped into the stilled lungs of the man on the bed, forcing them to work. Then the skipper sat down on the edge of the bed and waited for the victim to be called back from the precipice of the dead.

For a while, they sat in the shabby little attic room, all staring at the figure in the bed. Occasionally, the woman tore a sob from deep within her.

Finally, Hagerdon glanced at her. "You his wife?"

She made a vague, uncertain motion with her head which might have meant anything. "Is he going to—come back?"

For answer, Hagerdon switched to a second tank.

"He's coming out of it," he admitted. "I've just switched to the inhalator, and we'll let him breathe himself for a while to stimulate respiration. Now, what was his reason for suicide?"

Naughton saw her hesitate, then she said, slowly: "I haven't any idea. He hasn't been feeling well, I suppose. I called you when I smelled the gas leaking around the locked door."

Hagerdon met Naughton's eye. "Call the homicide, will you Todd? This is their grief."

As Naughton turned to the door, the woman threw herself in front of him. "No, wait. You mustn't call the cops."

Hagerdon frowned. "That's routine, lady. We got to notify the homicide squad on all attempted suicides."

She looked wildly from one to the other. "In the name of Heaven, don't call in the cops. It won't do no good!"

"I'm sorry," Naughton put in firmly. "Please let me pass."

She stiffened suddenly, and a small revolver appeared in her tremulous hand. "Back up. So help me, mister, I'll kill you before I'll let you call in any cops!"

Naughton frowned and estimated his chance of knocking the wicked little gun from her hand. It was Hagerdon who took the edge off the situation.

"All right," he grunted carelessly. "There's no use having a row about it. Forget it, Todd." He leaned forward and adjusted the valves. The resuscitator sputtered a couple of times, and Hagerdon moved to his feet, a nervous frown marring the even bronze mask of his face.

The woman let the gun fall to her side. "Is—is something gone wrong?" she managed.

Hagerdon turned his head toward Naughton, and one eye dropped in a perceptible wink. "Say, Todd, beat it down to the roadster and bring up another tank of oxygen. If there's not one there, run down to the corner drugstore."

The woman moved mechanically away from the door, the gun forgotten. "Hurry, hurry!" she pleaded.

Naughton hesitated, then passed into the corridor. He felt a little foolish at allowing the woman to bluff him, but he knew that Hagerdon did not want any trouble when he was working on a patient. Then, too, if Naughton took any active part in the case, he might be dragged into a court trial and taken from his own specialty. No, the matter was simply a routine case best handled by the homicide dicks.

He looked for a telephone on the way down, and, when he didn't find one, went outside. There was, as Hagerdon had suggested, a drugstore less than half a block down the street.

SERGEANT KANE answered the homicide's telephone, and Naughton winced when he heard the veteran's caustic voice. Then he smiled grimly, and said: "Hello, Sarge. This is Naughton. Captain Hagerdon asked me to call you. He found a guy with his head in an oven, and the gas on."

"Yeah?" Kane grunted. "Well, was the gas lit?"

"No, but at the mention of cops, the guy's wife—well, the woman who was with him, anyhow—pulled a gun. This is some of your grief."

"As if I ain't got nothin' else to do but run around after guys that want to kick themselves off! What am I—a wet nurse?"

"You'd know the answer to that one, Sarge," Naughton kidded.

"Yeah? Well, go to hell! Where's this monkey now?"

"Eight-three-four-two Shipland. Between Bronson and—"

A sudden detonation shook the booth, cutting off Naughton's words. A woman screamed somewhere else in the drugstore. Then a shattered windowpane crashed on the sidewalk outside.

"What the hell was that?" Kane demanded.

"An explosion," Naughton jerked. "Sounded like gas. Good-bye!" He banged up the receiver and charged out of the booth. As he ran for the street door, he could see people on the sidewalk starting to run north and a ghastly premonition of disaster constricted his diaphram.

The moment he hit the street, his worst fears were realized. One whole side of the rooming-house had been blown off, and flame enveloped the structure like a wrapper of scarlet cellophane.

Instinctively, Naughton began to run forward. Then he caught himself, went back to the corner in front of the drugstore and pulled the fire-alarm box. That done, he bolted for the blazing building. As if by magic, a crowd had formed in a morbid ring outside, and the flames illumined their curious, upturned faces.

The arson dick reached the front door, as several people in various undress fled to the street. He stepped aside to let the human flood roll by, searching their faces. Then he pushed inside and started up the stairs.

The second story stopped him. Smoke, black, treacherous, rolled down the corridor to attack him. He retreated before it. That advancing cloud was misted death, and Naughton had witnessed too many dead smoke-eaters to be reckless. Sick at heart, he backed down the stairs and out to the sidewalk.

The wailing caterwaul of sirens heralded the arrival of truck and engine companies from 23, and Naughton ran into the street to meet them. He shouted to clear the street, but the crazy shriek of the sirens did that and then, with a thunderous rumble, 23's gleaming pumper rocketed around the corner and pulled up beside the hydrant. Behind it, the hose-wagon slowed for the hydrant-man to drop off with a line, then blustered up to a stop in the street in front of the roaring structure. Before the lines were charged, a truck company splashed its red headlights down the pavement and came to a snorting stop beside the hose-wagon.

Naughton rushed up to the captain of the truck.

"For God's sake get a ladder up to top story," he rasped. "Wyatt Hagerdon's trapped up there."

Captain Mundy wasted no time in inquiry. He swung on his red-and-black helmeted crew, roaring: "Chute the forty-five to the fourth floor. Romp on it. Cap Hagerdon's up there!"

THE MEN needed no urging. In perfect evolution, they hauled out the great forty-five-foot ladder, pointed the top end toward the poles until the ladder was vertical. Then they lengthened it until the top end reached the fourth floor of the rooming-house. Even before the tip touched the sill, laddermen scrambled aloft.

Naughton started for the ladder, then paused. There would be little use trying to seek evidence of arson in that hell of flame and smoke. Somehow, he couldn't think clearly, knowing that Cap Hagerdon was up there. Had the explosion killed him?

Two official cars wailed up to the scene, adding to the din. Battalion Chief Hardesly piled out of his red roadster, and, in the car behind, Sergeant Kane and his partner, Kovack, arrived. They followed Hardesly over to where Naughton stood with Captain Mundy.

Hosemen overhauled their lines to both sides of the building. Mundy swept the scene with his eyes and shouted to his crew: "Ladder the west end of the building!" Then he turned to Hardesly. "Illuminating gas. She let go with an awful bang. Naughton tells me Hagerdon is up in the attic. I've— Gad, here they come now. Lively, boys, lend a hand there." This last was to his own men as he pointed aloft where a ladderman appeared through the little oval window with a limp figure draped over his shoulder.

A gasp went up from the crowd. Rescue! Hundreds of eyes followed the downward course of the fire-fighters and their inert burdens, and eager hands reached to relieve them as, black-faced, they grounded.

A slicker-clad man, with a red cross on his arm, stooped beside the two still forms of Hagerdon and the little bald-headed man.

Naughton swung on Mundy. "There's a woman up there," he shouted.

The ladderman, who had brought down the little man, shook his head. "Not up there. Just these two." He pointed to the pair on the ground.

Naughton frowned bewilderedly. Captain Mundy waved back the curious, with a sweep of his big arm. "Move away," he bellowed. "Give these men room. They'll need all the air they can get after being knocked out with that smoke."

The red-cross man came slowly erect. He gave Naughton a hard, direct stare, then said: "These two don't need air—they've been shot to death!"

Sergeant Kane shouldered his way to the speaker. "What's that?"

"These two men were shot to death," the examiner repeated. Kane glanced obliquely at Naughton, then dropped to his knees as if doubting the statement of the examiner. He made his own brief survey and looked up.

"Murdered. Naughton, you mentioned a woman with a gun."

The arson dick nodded dully. "Why, yes. But I don't think she—"

Kovack was shouting: "Hey, Sarge—that little guy! Ain't he—"

Kane silenced him with a disgusted scowl. "Sure it is." He returned his gaze to the arson dick. "You know this little guy, don't you, Naughton?"

Todd Naughton shook his head. "Never saw him until tonight."

"If you know who it is, Sergeant, say so," Hardesly snapped impatiently.

Kane gave the battalion chief a sidelong glance. "O.K. This little ape happens to be Deane Trasker, alias 'Matches,' one of the best torches who ever planned a touch-off! He got out of the state pen about two months ago after a ten-year arson rap."

CHAPTER TWO
FIND THE TORCH-WOMAN

NAUGHTON STARED down at the small corpse who, a decade before, had bedeviled the police and fire departments for nearly two years before he was finally caught and convicted. That was all before Naughton's time, but, although the arson dick had never seen Deane Trasker, he was familiar with his scarlet history.

"Well, there's the end of your recent incendiary fires, Naughton," Hardesly growled at last. "But what a hell of a price to pay." He went down on one knee beside the body of Hagerdon, removed his white helmet and whispered a brief prayer, while, in the street behind the big pumper, thundered an accompaniment, men cursed in hoarse voices and dirty spray misted his own white hair. Finally, he jerked erect, slapped on his helmet.

"Carry these men behind the lines," he barked.

Sergeant Kane took Naughton's arm and drew him away from the pounding pumper so that they might converse without shouting at each other. Kovack melted into the crowd after securing a description of the woman who had disappeared from the little attic room.

"Now, what the hell's this all about?" Kane demanded.

Naughton gave his head a regretful shake. "It looks like I blundered into something so hot it blew up in my face," he began ruefully, and outlined what had happened from the time he came out on the call with Hagerdon until the present moment. "Naturally, I didn't think the woman would kill Hagerdon and her man. I'd never have left if I had thought so. The newspapers will finish me. They'll say

I should have knocked the woman over myself, without leaving to call in you fellows. It's obvious now that's what I should have done."

"To hell with the newspapers!" Kane growled. "It wasn't your place to start a row, when Hagerdon was still workin' on the guy. But you should never even try to figure out what a dame's goin' to do because nobody can tell that—not even the dame herself."

"But why would she kill her man?"

"Maybe it seemed like a good idea at the time."

"Suppose it was someone else?"

Kane grimaced his disgust. "There you go off again—always tryin' to make a deep mystery out of a case. She was in the room, wasn't she? She didn't get singed? She had a gun an' threatened to blast you? Well, what in hell else do you want? Maybe you'd like her to walk in with the gun in her hand and confess?"

Naughton was saved from the necessity of a reply by the return of Detective Kovack, whose long, horse-face was warped into a puzzled frown.

Kane gave him an oblique glance. "Well, you act like you been kicked in the stomach. What's the matter?"

Kovack's bewilderment persisted. "You know who I just seen hangin' around? Mike Padgett."

The other's eyes slitted. "What was that shyster doin'?"

"Well, I asked him," Kovack admitted. "I says: 'Hi, Padgett, what you doin' so far from home? Interested in bonfires?' I says, just like that."

"All right," snapped Kane. "An what did he say?"

The big Pole hesitated, and something akin to a slow flush mounted his long features. "Well, Sarge, he says, snooty-like: 'When you can prove it's any of your damn business, I've got an office.'"

"An' you said?"

Kovack spread his hands. "Well, it took me a minute to sort of get that. It made me plenty sore, too. But by that time he'd moved away."

KANE SUCKED in a series of short breaths, preparatory to a verbal explosion, but he was still in the first stages of incoherent profanity when another man stalked over and hit him a slap on the back.

Kane glanced over his shoulder at the newcomer, exhaled wearily and growled: "Hello, Riley. You chasin' fire-engines, too?" He nodded toward the arson dick. "You know Todd Naughton. Jay Riley, a lousy private dick."

Naughton and Riley shook hands. "Heard plenty about you Naughton—all good," Riley said. "Did I walk into a private conference? The sergeant seemed either to be choking over a bone in his throat, or about to blow up."

"He was about to blow up," Kovack offered, then, as he caught Kane's lowering scowl, added hastily: "You chasin' fire-engines, the Sarge wants to know?"

Riley massaged his chin with a big hand. "Since Trasker is dead and any chance of a reward gone, I suppose you might as well have it," he admitted, after a pause. "I've been tailing him pretty close for the last couple of weeks. If this hadn't happened, I'd had him red-hot by this time tomorrow."

"If you've been trailing him," Naughton put in, "you must know something about the woman he was with. She was about thirty, slight, around one hundred and ten pounds."

Riley nodded. "Sure. That's Blanche Seabrook. He ran around with her before he went up this last time. Have you picked her up?"

Kane threw his hands up in a gesture of impatience. "We ain't picked anybody up. We just stand around an' gab like a lot of old women. A hell of a swell crew of dicks! One gets threatened by a dame with a gun—he goes an' calls the cops. The other sees a shyster practically ambulance-chasing an' takes a lot of lip without even tippin' his hat."

"He means me an' Mike Padgett. I ask Mike what he's doin' here and he—"

"Don't go over that yarn again, damn it!" shouted Kane.

Riley stopped smiling. "Wait a minute. Let's get this straight. You say Mike Padgett, the attorney, was around here tonight?"

"I seen him," Kovack reiterated.

"Well, so what?" growled Kane.

Riley said, "Humph," a couple of times. "It's strange," he said at length. "Matches Trasker was paroled to Padgett, at Padgett's request. The D.A. fought the move on the grounds that Padgett is a criminal attorney and, as a matter of fact, defended Trasker at his trial ten years ago."

Kane fingered the bulbuous tip of his red nose. "Gad, that's right! Mike Padgett nearly got himself disbarred over the case—bribed a witness, as I remember it."

"Then I betcha the dame will head for Padgett's office," contributed Kovack.

Kane's sarcastic rejoinder was interrupted by Naughton. "A moment ago, Riley, you said you were tailing Trasker. What's the rap?"

The private dick shrugged. "State Mutual, Texas Casualty, and a couple of the other companies that got nicked in this string of blazes, are old accounts of mine. They put up an awful squawk, so we been working night and day. I had a pretty strong case against Trasker, but I wanted to catch him red-handed. He got away from me late this afternoon, so I came over here to pick him up again. What worries me now is I got a tip he's planted a fuse in another hot one. If my accounts have another touch-off around this town tonight, I'll stand to lose some damn good customers."

"You think Trasker has arranged the plant for another touch-off?" Naughton wanted to know.

Riley heaved his shoulders again. "Well, he certainly went to a lot of trouble to give me the slip. I didn't figure he'd seen me, then he wandered into the subway terminal to buy a ticket. I tailed him onto an Eastbeach car, then, just as we neared Five Points, he got up and made for the front door. About four people got between me and the door, so he got off first. When the car stopped, a sedan swerved over and Trasker stepped from the street car into the sedan. He vanished just like that!" Riley snapped his fingers.

"Who was driving the sedan, or could you make 'em?" Kane asked.

"A dame. You see, they were gone before I got off the trolley, but, from the glimpse I got of her, I'd say it was this Seabrook wench. After I lost 'em, I went back to the office. I came over here on a chance they might show up. I guess I should have come right back here after they eluded me."

"Maybe this guy Padgett is in cahoots with Trasker?" submitted Kovack.

Riley grinned. "He's too smart to let you pin anything like that on him, Kovy. Still, it's funny he'd come out here tonight. And while I've tailed Trasker to Mike's office a couple of times, this is the first time Mike ever returned the visit that I know of."

"Ah, to hell with all this stuff!" Kane growled. "You tell me where I can pick up this Blanche Seabrook—that's all I want."

"Kovack's guess is as good as any," Riley admitted. "But I doubt if she'd be dumb enough to go direct to Mike's office. She's too smooth a squab for that." He glanced at Naughton. "Hardesly told me you were up in the room with Trasker and Cap Hagerdon. Was Trasker shot at that time?"

Naughton shook his head. "No. He had been gassed. We thought it was a suicide attempt. That's why I went to call Sergeant Kane. However, Hagerdon was bringing him out of it nicely."

"Did Trasker recover enough to say anything?" Riley asked.

Kane's angry snort interrupted Naughton's answer. "Cut it out, you two!" he shouted. "What's so complicated about it? Riley, you're as bad as Naughton! Just a couple of notoriety hounds. Come on, Kovy, let's get the hell out of here before I lose my good humor." He swiveled and stalked away over the web of hose-lines. With an apologetic grin, Kovack followed faithfully.

RILEY CHUCKLED. "Kane's a great guy, but there's no one else in the world who could work with him except that dumb Polish echo. At that, though, Kovy's a good, hard-working cop, and I've always suspected most of his stupidity is a pose to bolster up the sergeant's ego." He sobered, his face shadowed as the flames melted into thick, murky smoke. "What do you make of this set-up, Naughton?"

The arson dick stared moodily at the building, now under control of the smoke-eaters. "I don't know yet, but I hope you're right about Trasker being the torch on these recent touch-offs. I'm in a worse spot than you. Another good touch-off, and I'm through."

Riley nodded. "Yeah? Well, I don't think—"He stopped abruptly as a woman came stumbling toward them. A once-pert little hat was mashed on her disheveled curls, and, even in the dim, uncertain light of the street, the swelling around her right eye was visible. Other than that, she was a petite little blonde in her middle twenties.

"Oh, Jay," she gasped as she reached Riley. "She got away!"

Then she saw Naughton, as if for the first time, and closed her mouth with a sudden snap.

Riley took her arm to steady her. "Take it easy, kid," he said easily. "This is Todd Naughton of the Central Office Squad, so he's all right." To Naughton he introduced the girl. "This is my assistant, Miss Condon. She was covering the back of the house." He swung on the girl. "Now, Velma, what happened? You look like you tried to stop Seabrook and got slugged."

The blonde gave Naughton a wan smile, then frowned at Riley. The arson dick watched her eyes turn from brown to a metallic green.

"You called it," she snapped. "She must have been hiding close by because I picked her up on the fringe of the crowd. I tailed her into an alley about four blocks from here and she got me as I was passing a dark doorway. She must have worn a set of brass knuckles. Oh, my eye!" She put a slim hand over the swollen optic.

Riley laughed and gave her a good-natured pat on the shoulder. "Never mind, Velma, we both fumbled. Come uptown and I'll buy you a couple of steaks—one for the inside, and one for the out. Join us, Naughton?"

The arson dick shook his head. "Thanks, but I think I'll stick around. This joint is almost cool enough to enter, and I want to look it over. Glad to have met you, Miss Condon."

The girl glanced over her shoulder as they moved away. "The pleasure is reciprocated," she said in a low, husky voice. "I'm sorry you had to see me under such unfavorable conditions."

CHAPTER THREE
ASSASSIN FROM
THE ASHES

AFTER THEY had disappeared into the crowd, Naughton made his way over to the rooming-house. There was still a mixture of steam and smoke drooling out of the windows, and the whole building was heavy with that nauseating odor of burned cloth and rubber, but it had been pretty much of a flash fire, and, aside from the original damage of the explosion, and a brief charring, the old structure was fairly intact. The salvage crew were hard at work arranging catch-alls, tarps used as containers to catch the drip of water and preserve furnishings not already damaged by the flames.

The arson dick turned up the cuff of his trousers and waded up the narrow stairs. Sooty water dribbled down in a weak cascade, soaking his feet before he reached the second landing. He went up to the fourth floor, and, as he forced open the door of the little attic bedroom, he felt a sharp stab of conscience.

It was much the same as he had left it, except that smoke, water and flame had taken their toll. But, somehow, he was not conscious of the damage. He stared toward the blackened bed, and a bitter memory painted in the images of a man lying inert and a courageous Hagerdon forcing Death to relinquish her victim. Now, they were both dead, and he swung his gaze to the spot near the door where the woman had stood with the gun in her hand. Why, he asked himself, had she fired those fatal shots? Had Matches Trasker blurted out some secret—perhaps the secret of their incendiary activities—while in a semiconscious state? Despite the cynical observation of Sergeant Kane, Naughton felt there had to be some motive. Blanche Seabrook had been anxious enough to revive Trasker in the first place.

Unable to reach a satisfactory hypothesis, Naughton went out of the room and made his way down to the third floor. It was obvious that the kitchen had been the center of the explosion. The door was open, and he walked in to find a hose-man checking the place.

"Well, she was a hot one while she lasted," observed the fireman grimly.

The arson dick nodded. The stove was a twisted wreck.

"That must be a powerful gas to go up like that," Naughton commented. "I came in here, turned off the gas and opened the window about a full half hour before she went up."

The fireman looked up and wiped a gloved hand across his blackened features. "You must have turned it off in one of the other flats," he suggested. "This window was shut and locked, and all the gas-jets were wide open. Look, you can see for yourself." He pointed to the remains of the stove.

Frowning, Naughton went over. He examined the blackened, twisted pile of junk. The porcelain handles on the jets were cracked off, but, as the smoke-eater had declared, the jets were wide open. Even the window-sash, minus the glass, was locked down.

"There's another kitchen just like this one on the floor below," offered the fireman.

Naughton shook his head. "It was this kitchen," he insisted. "We found Trasker lying on that table." He indicated the blackened remains of a kitchen table propped precariously against the opposite wall. "Say, did you put that toaster there?" He crossed over and stared down at a seared wreckage of metal and wire that still stood on the table.

"Nothing's been touched in this room," the fireman said decisively. "If that's a toaster, it was on the table when the thing went up. What's the excitement, any how?"

"Pete, you stick around until the headquarters' photographer gets there, will you? I want this room left just as is. Get pictures taken of the window-sash, so as to show it was locked shut, and pictures of the stove with the open jets. Have 'em photograph this table and toaster from different angles. Then, when you're satisfied you've got pictures, bring the toaster into headquarters."

"Sure, I get it. This must be important, eh?"

"It's damned important," Naughton assured him. "Like I told you, I turned off those jets myself and opened one of those windows before I went out of this room. There was no electric toaster on that table then, because we had just lifted a man off it. That leaves only one explanation. Somebody came into this room after we took Trasker upstairs, closed and locked the windows and turned on the gas again. Later, when it got properly filled they ran in, plugged in the electric toaster, and beat it. An old-style toaster like this one would take a couple of minutes to get hot enough to ignite the gas, so the torch would have enough time for a getaway."

The fireman exhaled a respectful curse. "I get it now. The dame bumped off Trasker an' Cap Hagerdon, then beat it down here, plugged in the toaster an'—" He stopped talking, his eyes on the doorway. Someone stood there.

NAUGHTON SWUNG around to find a short, swart man framed in the opening. The latter met his hard stare, said: "So you found something—eh, Naughton?" He was truculent.

The arson dick frowned. "How did you get in here, Padgett?"

"I walked in," snapped the chunky man. "As one of the victims of this explosion was a former client of mine, what is the objection?"

"As a lawyer, you are probably aware there is a city ordinance against trespassing into a building that has been burned," Naughton pointed out. "By the way, when did you see Trasker last?"

"Why?"

"Well, I'm asking you."

Mike Padgett's bulldog chin jutted forward pugnaciously. "Listen, cop, if you're trying to pin this touch-off onto either Deane Trasker or myself, forget it."

"I asked you a question," Naughton reminded the lawyer.

"And I didn't answer it, nor do I intend to. If you feel sure enough of yourself to pinch me, go to it. But be damn sure before you try it. Meanwhile, go peddle your apples somewhere else."

"A tough guy, eh?" observed the fireman.

"A criminal lawyer," Naughton corrected him. "That's how he develops such a big mouth." He turned back to Padgett. "I asked you a civil question, and you get wise. All right, smart guy, absorb a load of this. When I'm ready to make a pinch, I'll make it without your advice. Meanwhile, don't make your wisecracks too personal. I don't have to take 'em. Now, get the hell out of here before I take you in for trespassing."

The weird reflected light in the blackened room filled the deep lines of the lawyer's face with shadows. He opened his mouth, then abruptly changed his mind about speaking and stalked out of the room. Naughton listened until the other's steps clumped down the stairs, then he swung back to the fireman.

"Keep everybody out of this room until you get those pictures," he warned. "Especially guys like that last one."

HE WENT into the corridor, and, with the aid of his flashlight, made his way through the debris to the rear of the building. Cursing softly, he remembered now that the Seabrook woman had remained below when he and Hagerdon had taken Trasker to the fourth floor. She had had time, in the interval prior to her appearance in the attic room, to re-close the window and open the jets.

At the end of the hallway, he found a tiny, inclosed stairway leading to the ground floor, and followed down until he passed into a small yard. Going through the muddy inclosure, he walked into an alley which, he decided, must have been the place where Riley's blond assistant had picked up Blanche Seabrook.

The trail of the girl, of course, was hopelessly cold now, so he decided to circle the block and ride back to Station 23 on one of the trucks. He switched off his flash, pocketed it, and started for the street a half black north. The moon had come up, yet not sufficiently to clear the buildings which lined the cobbled alleyway. But the sky was bright, and the blackness of the shadows softened the squalor of the neighborhood.

The first shot took Naughton by surprise. It whined past his shoulder and plunked into a metal garbage can piled on a barrel. Naughton was diving for the cobblestones, when the next three slugs whined overhead.

A strange atavistic elation swept over Todd Naughton. Here was something he could sink his teeth in, somebody tangible to cope with. He rolled on his side, swung out his service .38 and propped himself up on one elbow. All he wanted just now was a target—and the score of Cap Hagerdon's death would be settled with a grim finality.

But no target appeared, and, as the seconds lengthened into minutes, Naughton had a sinking feeling that his assailant was putting plenty of distance between them. He strained his eyes to pierce the gloom and tried desperately to conceive a human shape out of the silhouetted piles of rubbish. At last he rose, cautiously, ready to swap lead at the first sign of encouragement. Nothing happened, and he moved forward to explore.

The shots had followed each other with such rapidity that Naughton never knew just where they came from. He presumed, and it seemed most logical, that the would-be killer had stood on the other side of the high board fence. But there were no clues to be found in the darkness. Angry and feeling a little foolish, the arson dick tramped around the block to the front of the ancient rooming-house. The fire over, the crowd had disappeared as magically as it formed, and now only weary firemen remained to load their dirty equipment back on the trucks.

Naughton stood on the fringe, taking it in. Then Battalion Chief Hardesly spotted him and started to come over. Naughton knew what to expect and meant to avoid it. Pretending he didn't see the sour old smoke-eater, he turned casually away. A hovering taxi caught his eye, and he made a grab for it. As he dove into the welcome haven of the tonneau, he barked his directions.

"Headquarters—and romp on it!"

CHAPTER FOUR

SHADOW ON A DOOR

IT WAS a few minutes after midnight when Naughton slipped into Central Station through a rear door and sidled down the empty corridor to his own cubbyhole of an office, unobserved. He wanted a few moments alone with his files so that he might check over his records and do a little heavy thinking. It seemed as if the whole ghastly business were but a mirage, a phony reflection of a hidden truth. But solitude was not to be his, for he had barely time to take from his file the folder on professional arsonists now known to be in the city, when a shadow suddenly formed on the translucent glass of the door. Naughton sighed grimly, as the door swung inward and the hull of Sergeant Kane ferried through the opening with his partner, Kovack, in tow.

Kane sauntered over to the desk and rested one hip against a corner. He was a heavy, squat man with a barrel-trunk and short, stubby legs. To strangers, he gave the impression of a sloppy fat man, but that was a dangerous illusion. Kane was hard, alert and cat-fast on his big feet, but it amused him to fool people so he furthered the deception by assuming a lazy, indolent pose. Naughton suspected that the sergeant's bad temper was also a part of his act, but, be that as it may, in times of tension Kane did get on Todd Naughton's nerves.

Kovack was everything that Sergeant Kane was not. Tall, lanky and apparently half stupid, it was his tiresome habit to repeat whatever statement Kane had made, regardless of its relevancy. The dicks referred to him as Kane's Polish Echo. But, as Riley had remarked, Kovack was a pretty good dick. Whether by brains or luck, he usually turned up at the right moment in a crisis, although at the time he invariably made it look like a blunder.

"I'm supposed to be off duty by this time," Kane crabbed at Naughton. "But the fire department's putting up an awful howl about Cap Hagerdon getting it. Me'n Kovy'll have to keep goin' until we pick up this Seabrook dame that did the shooting. By the way, the Old Man was askin' about you, kid. He's got ants in his pants."

Naughton exhaled wearily. "I guess it'll be brass buttons and a beat in the sticks for me," he admitted. "I wish I'd recognized Trasker when I first saw him on that table."

"Well, your troubles would have been over," Kane agreed. "Now, what I came in for was to see what you had on this Seabrook squab."

Naughton thumbed his folder to the S's and scanned the list. "Not a damn thing," he acknowledged. "She isn't even listed."

Kane swore. "Well, what did she say? Was she livin' with Trasker? You must have got some information!"

"She wanted him to live—wanted it pretty desperately," Naughton said. "Also, she didn't want the cops brought into it."

"I'd hate to have a dame want me to live like that," Kovack contributed. "With a sweetheart like that around, a guy wouldn't never need no enemies."

"Wisecrackin' again," snarled Kane. "This ain't no time for levity!" To Naughton he went on: "We'll find out why she killed him after we pinch her. The whole trick now is to get the dame."

"What about Padgett?" Naughton asked. "He came pussy-footing into the house after you fellows left, and, when I questioned him, he got tough as hell."

"Mike Padgett is an A-number-one, first-class heel," Kane growled. "He's also a criminal lawyer. He's probably mixed up in the ring. But he isn't the guy that killed Hagerdon, an' that's what interests me. I want that dame."

"Maybe, like I said, she'll head for Padgett's office," Kovack offered.

"Use your head!" flamed Kane. "Give the dame credit for some brains. She'd expect some dummy like you to think of Padgett's office, so do you think she's goin' to bust into a trap? Be your age, Kovy. That dame is goin' to hole up somewhere and maybe get in touch with Mike. Since we can't find anything here, we better go out to—" He stopped, as the door opened, and Jay Riley came in.

"I suspected I'd find you all here," Riley greeted them. "Any news of Blanche?"

Kane shook his head. "We're goin' out to Padgett's home and maybe pick up his trail. I figure she'll get in touch with Mike right away. Have you got anything?"

"Not a thing," Riley admitted. "I contacted a couple of stoolies, but Trasker's been playing 'em close against the vest since he's been out. I think your idea is a good one. She may be out working on another touch-off."

Kane opened the door. "Well, come on you guys. How about you, Naughton? You better come along with us."

Naughton relaxed in his chair. "It won't take over six hundred pounds of beef to capture Blanche Seabrook," he grinned ruefully. "You three guys can handle it."

"You better come," Kovy reiterated.

"Aw, t'hell with him," Kane rasped. "Let him stay here an' sulk." He stamped out of the office, and, grinning, the other pair followed.

NAUGHTON WATCHED the closed door for several minutes. Then he rose, lighted a cigarette and went over to the grimy little window that looked out into the court below. There was a deep, brooding silence, hanging over the city, that stirred him. But it passed suddenly when a distant street car clanged for a crossing and other nocturnal vehicles added their individual noises to the night sounds of the great city.

He mused over what had been said. Kane didn't believe that Blanche Seabrook would head for Padgett's office because she was too wily a criminal. A killer, Sergeant Kane reasoned, would be too smart for that. But suppose Blanche Seabrook had killed in the heat of an unbalancing emotion, or suppose, even, that she was not the real killer. In that case, perhaps she might do the obvious thing.

He fingered through the pages of the telephone directory until he found *Padgett, Michael Q.* The address was 614 Harcourt Building. He took a last deep inhalation of the cigarette, stubbed it out in an ash-tray and sidled into the corridor. He left the station as he had entered it, by the unobtrusive rear door.

A cruising cab shuttled him across mid-town, and he abandoned it at the intersection of Eighth and Sutter.

After that, he walked the intervening distance and took up a furtive position in a vaulted doorway directly across the street from the Harcourt Building wherein Michael Q. Padgett maintained a business office.

The twelve-story structure looked placid, sleepy. A dim, subdued night-light spotted the front, suggestive of scrub-women going their early-morning rounds, or clerks, struggling through the night after a balance.

Naughton shifted his weight from one foot to the other, as he waited. Every five or six minutes a street car banged square-wheeled over the track crossing at the intersection. After a half hour of it, Naughton was able to tell the direction of the noise-making trolley, by the sound. Then an owl-bus droned past his spot, cutting off his vision of the arched entrance across the street.

The bus did not stop, so the woman could not have been on it, but the instant the big conveyance rolled by, she was there hurrying along the opposite sidewalk, head held low. The arson dick knew it was Blanche Seabrook even before the wan light of the building entrance splashed her white face. Where she had come from, he didn't know. One moment the street had seemed deserted, the next she was there before him. His first impulse was to stop her, but, on second thought, he allowed her to enter the Harcourt Building, unmolested. If she were tied in with Mike Padgett, Naughton wanted to know about it. There was no point in getting individual criminals if the brains, system and organization behind them were permitted to continue unmolested.

As he moved out of his hiding-place, and edged across the street, through the bronze and glass doors he could see the night-watchman usher her into an elevator. When the elevator doors clanged shut, Naughton sidled into the foyer and stood in the shadow of a pillar, watching the arrow of the indicator arc its way up to the 6. It paused there a moment, then started to swing down. Naughton ducked for the dim-lit stairs and took them two at a time.

The Harcourt Building was not new. The corridors were narrow and a trifle dingy. Naughton topped the sixth flight, hesitated to make sure the marble-lined corridor was deserted, then he tiptoed up and made his way along it. Number 614 was directly opposite the white, wire-filled glass doors of the elevator shaft. Under the numerals, the translucent-glass panel bore the legend, *Michael Q. Padgett, Attorney at Law*, etched in sharp silhouette by the lights, of the office beyond. Naughton, glanced both ways, then moved close to the door.

PADGETT'S VOICE came to him, husky, vibrant. "You did the only smart thing, babe, and you did your best to give him a break. But the heat's on now—plenty. The cops are looking for you. Better take a powder until it blows down."

The girl had apparently been sobbing, for when she spoke, her voice was edged, barely under control. "I know—I know. I should have killed that damned Velma Condon."

"How did you shake her?" Padgett wanted to know.

"I hit her once, and she went down. Then a fireman came around the edge of the building, and I ran. But listen, Mike, what about that other touch-off?"

"You better let well enough alone and clear out, babe. With you out of the way, I can take care of things."

"And let that Acme Drug warehouse—" Her words were interrupted by the sudden hum of the ascending elevator.

Naughton swore softly, turned. He glimpsed the lights in the office go out and he stood, hating to move for fear his footsteps on the hard marble would give him away. The elevator rumbled up, and, to his intense relief, passed without stopping. He heard it pause somewhere above, then descend, and he heaved a sigh of pleasure when the elevator painted the glass doors with light and passed from sight below.

Apparently the passage of the lift brought relief to the inmates of the office, for the lights again flamed on the inside, and Padgett commented: "Well, that gave me a start, babe. I'd hate to have anyone walk in on us when we got all this dough spread out and not even a popgun to defend ourselves."

"You can sit there, Mike," the Seabrook woman said harshly. "I'm going."

Naughton heard her cross the room, and then her shadow formed on the glass panel. He unholstered his gun, braced himself, and, when she opened the door, he was ready. He gave her a quick push that sent her reeling back into the office and jumped inside, his gun swinging toward the desk where he had first heard Padgett's voice.

In the action-packed moment that followed, Naughton knew he had walked into trouble. Padgett was not at the desk, and, as the arson dick's eyes flicked to the woman crouched against a chair, he knew he was in for it. He started to turn, then to duck as he saw an arm swinging toward him. He glimpsed the contorted features of Michael Q. Padgett, heard the Seabrook girl scream: "Don't, Mike!" Then something solid collided with his chin, and consciousness was blotted out by the explosion in his head.

CHAPTER FIVE
THREE-ALARM TOUCH-OFF

TODD NAUGHTON came out of it slowly. At first he could not figure out just where he was. He tried to turn over, only to discover that his right wrist was securely shackled to an immovable radiator near the window. A hasty check of his pockets with his left hand proved what he dreaded—he was manacled with his own cuffs and his keys were gone. He sat and swore, while his aching eyes searched the place.

The scene whipped alive his memory. Of course it was the office of Mike Padgett. He could read the name backward on the dimly translucent panel of the door. There was no light in the spacious room save the reflected moonlight which seeped through the windows. Naughton looked at his wrist-watch, but it had broken in his fall—it could hardly have been called a fight. He wondered about the time, and cold sweat formed on his forehead as he recalled the words of Blanche Seabrook. The Acme Drug!

He thought of shouting, in the hope that the elevator man would hear him. But that would waste time in futile explanations.

His badge, gun and all evidence of authority, had been removed from his person, so the watchman would probably call in some harness-bull and Naughton would be arrested. There was no surmising what might happen in the interim.

There was only one other way out of it, and Todd Naughton took it reluctantly. By practically standing on his head, with one toe he could just manage to reach the telephone on the desk. He tried twice before he succeeded in raking it onto the floor in such a manner that the extension wire came within reach of his free hand. The operator was excitedly demanding the number, when he finally snapped the words: "Police headquarters!" When the police operator came on the wire, Naughton grimly asked for Sergeant Kane in the homicide.

Kovack answered the phone.

"This is Naughton, Kovack. Where's Kane?"

"Him and Riley's gone across the street to the Dutchman's for a slug of Java. Say, where you been? The Old Man was asking—"

"Shut up and listen," Naughton growled. "Bring a Peerless handcuff key and an extra gun and come up to Office Six-fourteen in the Harcourt Building, on Eighth, just beyond Sutter."

"Yeah. Say, ain't that Mike Padgett's office? Say, I'll bet I was right. I'll bet you went up there on my tip an' captured the Seabrook—"

"I didn't capture anyone," Naughton stopped him. "I'm sitting on the floor shackled to a radiator. So will you stop arguing and come down here?"

"Well, why don't you unlock yourself? What's the idea? Say, here's the sarge now." His voice faded slightly as he turned his mouth away from the instrument, but not sufficiently for Naughton to miss his words. "Hey, Sarge, it's Naughton! He captured himself up in Mike Padgett's office. He wants—" There was the sound of a heavy body moving violently, then Kane's voice boomed over the wire.

"Hello, Naughton. Kane. What's this crazy stuff?"

Naughton swore. "Listen. Will you hurry down here with an extra handcuff key? Don't ask questions. Send a squad of men out to the Acme Drug warehouse on Front

Street. There's going to be a touch-off out there. That's where Padgett and the Seabrook woman are heading. Send out a general order to pick 'em up. Make it snappy."

Sweating with recrimination, Naughton slumped on the floor beside the radiator, and glared hopefully at the door. What a sap! The lonely elevator made a trip up and showed him how he had been discovered by Padgett and the girl. They had turned out the lights when they heard the elevator ascend and then, sitting in semi-darkness, as Naughton was at this moment, they had seen his figure silhouetted against the frosted panel of the door by the moving lights of the elevator. The rest had been easy. They had baited him into the room with talk of money, and Blanche Seabrook's remark, "You can sit there, Mike!" had been a clever piece of psychological deception. She had reasoned that Naughton would instinctively swing his attention to the desk, whereas, in reality, Mike Padgett had stood just inside the door waiting to slug him.

NAUGHTON'S INTROSPECTION was interrupted by the vibrant hum of the rising elevator. It stopped at the sixth, the doors clanged and the glass panel on the office door glowed, then a bulky shadow-evolved against it, and, a moment later, someone tried the knob. Naughton heard Kane say: "It's locked. Maybe this is a gag."

"It's no gag," Naughton called wearily. "Get a key from the watchman."

After a brief argument in the hall, the door swung inward. Kane's great bulk was framed in the opening for a moment while he groped for a panel switch. Then, light. Kane, Kovack and a scared old watchman stood there.

The sergeant glared at Naughton sitting on the floor, his right arm shackled to the intake pipe of the radiator, then he broke into a loud guffaw. "Say, that's a riot! Gad, I wish I had a camera—eh, Kovy?"

Kovack snickered obligingly. "Yeah, we wish you had a camera, Sarge."

"O.K., I earned it," Naughton grimaced. "Rub it in."

Kane crossed the room in three strides. He had had his little joke; now he was all business. As he knelt beside Naughton and fitted a key into the blue-steel cuffs, he said: "All right, kid. I sent the pick-up order over the air and the teletype. Vance is taking a squad out to the Acme. Now, what's the score?"

Naughton scrambled to his feet, crossed to a water-cooler and took a long drink. Putting the glass down, he turned and detailed what had happened.

He had rather expected a ribbing from the irascible sergeant, but Kane only said: "That was a good hunch of yours—coming up here. Incidentally, I dug up a little dope on the gal. She was married to Trasker. Yeah, I figured that'd surprise you. They were married by the same judge who sentenced Trasker, and she's waited all these years for him. Funny she'd kill him, now ain't it?"

"That baby must be plenty tough," Kovy interjected.

"Well, she knew what she was doin'," Kane decided. "She'd been married before to a guy named Seabrook who was killed in an accident a couple of days after their wedding. But I don't get the connection with Mike Padgett. Well, let's blow out to the Acme and see if Vance picked up anything. I told him to call here—"

As the phone jangled, Kane reached for it. "That's probably Vance now. Hello... Yeah, this is Kane. What did you find, Vance?" He listened a moment, and his face hardened. He shot an oblique glance at the arson dick. "We're on our way." He pronged the receiver.

"They miss 'em?" Naughton wanted to know.

Kane pulled out a service revolver and handed it to Naughton, saying: "The Acme warehouse blew the lid off about five minutes ago, and Vance tells me it's giving the best imitation of hell-fire at this minute that he ever saw."

Naughton dove for the hallway. "Let's go—"

He climbed in the rear seat with Kane and stared over the square right shoulder of Kovack through the windshield where the explorative beams of the headlights splashed and bounced on the fog-damp pavement. For all his dim-brain poses, the big Pollack could push a fast-wagon through traffic with the careless ease of a trick bicycle-rider. As he swung onto Market, Kovack kneed on the siren and held the swaying police-car to the middle of the tracks. The rear ends of street cars, taxis, trucks, seemed to leap up at him. But just when, to Naughton in the rear seat, a crash seemed inevitable, Kovack gave the siren an extra scream and rolled around the obstruction with split inches to spare. It was pure art of its kind.

But the caterwauling of the siren cut out other noises, and, on swinging onto Front Street they almost collided with a hurtling ladder-truck whose siren also prevented the helmeted driver from hearing the police machine. Kovy yanked the wheel, and the squad-car slued sidewise into a sickening dry skid. For nearly twenty feet they slid, and, so close it was, the left rear fender of the sedan was torn off by a brush with the powerful truck. But Kovack fought them out of the skid and wound up in the gutter, the police-car stalled, facing the way it had come. He glanced over his shoulder and favored his passengers with a foolish smile.

"Listen, you stumblebum," Kane said. "Vance only said it was a hell of a fire, not that we had to go to hell to see it. Now, keep your addresses straight. Will this buggy run?"

"Oh, sure," Kovack chuckled. "If you think that was close, you oughta seen the time—"

"You're damn right I thought that was close," Kane interrupted savagely. "Now, get rolling."

Kovy U-turned the sedan and proceeded on his way.

THE ACME WHOLESALE DRUG warehouse stood in the middle of the block. There was a small yard on the north side of the building protected by a seven-foot board fence topped by two strands of barbed wire. The south side was taken up by a private spur track that cut diagonally across Front Street went through a cyclone-wire gate and entered the warehouse for unloading. The structure was old and of brick facing, but Naughton knew that the underwriters had regarded the long, six-story warehouse as a fire-trap for years.

They parked the sedan back of the already established firelines and moved up close. As Vance had forewarned them, it was a hot one. Vance himself surged out of the crowd and joined them. Riley was with him.

"Well, Sarge, she sure went up in a hurry!"

"Was it an explosion?" Naughton asked Riley.

Riley shrugged. "It must have been to get such headway although it was well under way before we arrived. I was with the Sarge when your call came in, and I took it with Vance. What happened?"

NAUGHTON GRUNTED, stared up at the blazing building. The fire had started low, probably in the basement, and was working upward behind a screen of smoke.

The lower three floors were seething infernos, and spasmodically came the dull boom-boom of bottled chemicals exploding. The arson dick winced. He knew the dangers the fire-fighters would encounter in this touch-off, for there was no way of anticipating what might happen. Explosions, deadly gases, flashes of liquid flame.

"I went up to Padgett's office," Naughton admitted in answer to Riley's query.

"I walked into a trap, and Mike slugged me."

"How'd you learn about this touch-off? This was about what I feared, you know."

Naughton nodded glumly. "I remember you forecast something of the sort. They were discussing it when I got to Mike's office. He wanted the girl to lam but she insisted on coming down here. Any sign of them?"

The screaming of sirens heralded the arrival of the three-alarm companies.

"I threw a cordon around the block," Vance offered. "But they would have had plenty time to get away before we got here."

Kane bobbed his head decisively. "Hell, yes! They probably had this joint all cased and planted a week ago, then, after they slugged you, they came down and put the match to it."

"That's right," Riley contributed. "Trasker undoubtedly had all the fuses planted so that all the Seabrook gal had to do was touch it off. Like I said, I had a tip he was up to something like this, but I couldn't find out where it was. Well, I know now. One of my best accounts, and this puts me right back of the eight-ball."

A uniformed cop came charging through the crowd and panted to a floundering stop in front of Kane.

"Hey, Sarge! There's a dame trapped up in there!" He pointed toward the fourth story of the doomed structure. "Some guy saw her at a side window—she screamed for help. Then she disappeared!"

Kane shot a quick glance at his companions. "Go tell that to Battalion Chief Hardesly!" he shouted at the informant. "Come on, Kovy, we'll beat it around there. You guys better take the south end." This last to Naughton and Riley. "Maybe we got a break!"

Riley swung around and started off at a dead run, Naughton at his side. "Boy, I sure hope so!" the private op panted. "If we could just nail Mike and that jane, maybe I could hold my accounts."

The arson dick grunted, and, together, they ducked through the railway gate and worked their way east toward the rear of the warehouse. Glancing back over his shoulder, Naughton glimpsed the eager faces of the huge crowd, hushed, awed, painted in shifting, variegated colors by the dancing flames. With a snort of disgust, he turned back to his objective.

CHAPTER SIX
FLAME-FIEND

AT THE back of the spur, it was quieter, for a dim block of freight cars, hunched like frightened sheep, seemed to absorb most of the din and confusion that existed in the street out front. But Naughton and Riley could still hear the rumbling of the flames, like the belly-chuckles of some Gargantuan demon. The side wall of the warehouse was most blank with an occasional window breaking the bareness. They were two thirds of the way back when glass crashed on the ground before them. Naughton swore, jumped back and looked up the wall. Riley spat a soft oath.

In the shattered frame of a window, four stories above them, appeared the torso of a man. He leaned far out, as if to escape the little wisps of smoke that stole around his body.

"For God's sake, help us!" he shrieked.

"It's Mike Padgett!" Naughton gasped short by the snarl of a gun at his elbow.

The man in the window made a queer, convulsive jump. For a split instant, it looked as if he would topple through the window, then he suddenly sagged back out of sight.

"What in hell—" began Naughton angrily.

"That's one torch who isn't going to get away!" Riley snarled. "We could convict the girl on your testimony, but we had nothing on that skunk except a moral certainty."

"The girl's in there!"

Riley holstered his gun. "You stick here and watch. I'll go get a rescue crew." He swiveled and plunged into the shadow of the freight cars on his way to the street.

Naughton frowned, watched Riley disappear. He turned his eyes back to that black hole where Padgett had been. Probably Mike deserved to die, but— He shook off the sensation of censure that gripped him. This was no time for sentiment.

Yet, a gnawing suspicion kept urging him to action. He glanced toward the street, but still no ladder-crew appeared. Could something have happened to Riley? He started for the front of the building, then changed his mind and ran to the rear.

As he half expected, there was an ancient fire-escape zigzagging down the back end of the warehouse. But, to his intense disappointment, it stopped off sheer, some fifteen feet above the ground level. For a moment, he was stumped, then a desperate plan came to him. He peeled off his coat and ran to a telephone pole that was located about ten feet from the fire-escape.

He climbed it until he reached a height about five feet above the level of the first landing of the fire-escape. He angled around, so that the pole was at his back, and he balanced, heels hooked over the pole-spikes, hands behind him.

Then he jumped.

He crashed heavily, tearing a long gash in his pants and cracking his elbow on the wire railing. He clung there a moment, then slowly drew himself to safety. He scrambled up to the fourth floor and found a metal-covered door barring his progress. From a pocket, he extracted a long knife with a special razor-thin blade. He forced the steel into the crack of the door just above the lock, and, after a couple of minutes of manipulation, the door surrendered, and Todd Naughton found himself facing a long, black corridor rapidly filling with smoke.

Pocketing the knife, Naughton took out a small flash. Then, covering his face with a handkerchief, he ducked inside.

He stood in darkness, orienting himself before he groped his way forward. Long training in the observance of details told him how far was the window—where he had seen Padgett—from the rear of the building. He counted off the paces, cautiously feeling his way through the fog of smoke until finally the meager beam of his flashlight found a door. He eased inside, saw the window and the tableau beside it.

ETCHED IN the tired circle of light was the inert body of Padgett, and, on her knees beside him, crouched Blanche. She stared blankly into the blinding light then brought up a gun. Naughton cleared the intervening space and smashed the weapon from her hand.

"You little hellion. You don't care how many men you murder."

"I—I thought you were Jay Riley."

"So you got it in for Riley, eh?"

She wheeled to her feet like a cat, panting before him. "Got it in for him? He killed my husband, tried to murder me, and now he's killed my brother."

Smoke was rapidly seeping into the room, and Naughton's eye ached. But he suddenly lost all sense of time or place.

"What's that you said? Riley killed Trasker, Padgett, your brother?"

She faced him, and, in the weird reflected light, her eyes glowed with a half-mad glint of truth.

"You're the fool," she screamed at him. "You work right along with a crooked, double-crossing murderer. Riley killed my husband, he killed Mike, and he'll kill you if he finds out you know. Certainly, Mike was my brother—why do you think he had Deane paroled to him but to help me—us? You think we set this blaze, don't you—you stupid fool? Well, we didn't. Riley had this touch-off all arranged as part of his frame against Deane Trasker. Mike and I came down here to try and stop it, but we were trapped. Mike sprained his leg, and we couldn't escape. Now, you know, idiot, but we'll never get out of here to prove it."

"But why should Riley frame Deane Trasker?"

"It's Riley who has been firing all these plants," she sobbed. "When he heard about Deane being paroled, he saw a chance to frame a goat and clean up the cases. He approached Deane and offered him an undercover job trying to find out who was responsible for these fires. Mike and I pleaded with Deane not to have anything to do with Riley, but Deane wanted to stand on his own feet. Well, it didn't take him long to smell a rat, so he shadowed Riley a couple of times and got the set-up. He was just about ready to take the whole mess to the district attorney when Riley found out, somehow. Riley and that terrible Condon woman came up to the apartment when I was out, and beat him unconscious. Then they put his head in the oven to make it look like a suicide. I stumbled in at the wrong moment and they beat me and locked me in a closet.

"I got out and called the fire department. I should have told the truth, but I was afraid Riley would blast his side of the story and nobody would believe Deane because he was an ex-convict. When you went out of our room, Riley and that woman came back. They murdered Deane and the fireman and took me away so they could torture the truth out of me. I broke away and—"

"You've said quite enough," came a voice from the doorway.

Naughton glimpsed the outline of Jay Riley in the open doorway, then he dragged the girl to the floor as the private dick's gun roared. As he went down, Naughton jerked out his own gun.

"Hold it, Riley."

Riley's answer came sharply from the muzzle of his gun. Naughton shoved the girl hard, rolled over twice and snapped on his light. Simultaneously, he fired, once—twice. Riley pirouetted, then one leg doubled and he spiraled to the floor.

Billows of thick smoke rolled over the dead man in the doorway and flooded the room. Naughton stumbled to his feet and beat his way toward the window. He broke out the few jagged edges of glass and fired three shots in quick succession. He was trying to gauge the risk of a drop when he saw running figures cross the spur-yard below. Then the booming voice of Kane brought relief.

"That you kid?"

"For God's sake, shoot a ladder up here," Naughton coughed out.

Someone shouted, "Coming right up!" and the arson dick saw six laddermen run into position with a long forty-five foot extension. He didn't wait to see it rise. Instead, he sucked in a deep breath and turned back to the girl.

He switched on his light and saw her on the floor again, her arms around the body of Padgett. Naughton swung his light, and it found a grim reflection in the sightless eyes of Riley—dead in the doorway. Naughton turned to the window, just as a fireman thrust his head inside.

"Come on Naughton. This wall won't last much longer."

He bent swiftly and lifted Blanche to his shoulders. She surrendered apathetically, and he managed, with the aid of the fireman, to stagger through the window and onto the ladder. Eager hands reached up to help him as he neared the ground.

A COUPLE of minutes later, two laddermen grounded the bodies of Padgett and Riley. Kane swore: "By Gad, we got Padgett. He's still alive. But they got poor old Jay Riley!"

"I got Riley," Naughton explained quietly, and told the story.

When Naughton had finished, the sergeant smacked his lips. "We can pick up the Condon tart, get her to fill in the gaps, and we got our cases all in the bag."

Detective Kovack nodded approvingly.

"Yes, sir. Say, by the way, ain't any of you guys hungry?"

"If Kovy was an undertaker, he'd eat himself to death," Kane's face soured in disgust. "Every time he sees a stiff, it whets his appetite. Maybe he's part cannibal."

"Maybe I am," Kovy grinned. "I got a cousin what's a auto-racer. They've named him what you called me—Cannonball Kovack."

ABOUT THE AUTHOR

L **ES WHITE** would rather sail a boat than eat; he'd
rather fly a plane than sail a boat; and he'd rather
write good fiction than do any of these. We've asked him
this month, as author of the complete novel, "Flight to
Nowhere," to tell our *Argosy* readers some more about
himself Leslie T. White—Born Ottawa, Canada, May 12,
1903. Came to the United States when I was twelve. Quit
school at fourteen to work in a machine shop. Wanted to
be a cartoonist; worked at a score of jobs, such as truck
driving, printers devil, stock clerk, draftsman, etc. Joined
the Cameron Highlanders, served eighteen months. After
army, knocked around with a carnival one summer, then
tried firing on the railroad. I shoveled enough coal on the
Grand Trunk, now absorbed by the Canadian National
Railways, during one winter to heat hell for five years. Back
to the States again I eventually landed a job as a ranger,
and developed my old hobby of photography to a degree
where I was able to work for Mary Pickford during the
shooting of *Little Annie Rooney*. The next ten years are
covered in my autobiography, *Me, Detective* (Harcourt
Brace 1936). I worked during that time as a criminal
deputy sheriff in Ventura, California, going to the Los
Angeles District Attorney's office as chief identification
expert. I've dabbled in a lot of things. I studied lion train-

ing under Hermann Zeigler. I spent a winter in the sub-arctic with the Royal Canadian Mounted Police. I took flying and got my license. I studied navigation. An old partner and pal of mine is now warden of the allegedly toughest penitentiary in the country, Folsom. I spend a lot of time with him and the boys, I travel a lot. Over sixty thousand miles in the last couple of years, most of it in South America, where I acquired my marmoset, Ivan the Terrible (see picture) I keep moving because the reading public demands accuracy and realism.